GALOS; Z J

WANDERING THE CITY TRAILS

Book II

Pilgrimage and Rebirth

Impressum

Bibliographical information of the German National Library. The German National Library indexes this publication with the German National Bibliography. Detailed bibliographical data may be derived from the Internet website: http://dnb.dnb.de

Publisher: BoD · Books on Demand GmbH,
In de Tarpen 42, 22848 Norderstedt, bod@bod.de
Print: Libri Plureos GmbH, Friedensallee 273,
22763 Hamburg

ISBN: 978-3-7693-2889-9

Pilgrimage is a powerful metaphor for any journey
with the purpose of finding something that matters
deeply to the traveller.

Phil Cousineau

Shorten my days thou canst with sullen sorrow,
And pluck nights from me, but not lend a morrow;
Thou canst help time to furrow me with age,
But stop no wrinkle in his pilgrimage.

William Shakespeare

Everything touches everything.

Jorge Luis Borges

Acropolis of Athens. Parthenon East Façade Detail

Wandering along known paths of Athens
Pilgrimage and Rebirth

Epilogue.

I have been accommodated in a single-roomed apartment, which I call a bedsitter, in the suburb of Kynosargous in Athens, sometimes known as Kinossargous. Translated, it also means where the dog is buried, and I recall in my early teens the saying in German, 'wo der Hund begraben ist'.

Perhaps, as the phrase is related to mythology when Herakles was banned from the centre of Athens because he was considered a bastard and had his gymnasium in Kynosargous, perhaps 'the dog buried' is related to his ancestry and the facts about his parents.

Herakles was my childhood hero. My aunt, my mother's sister, had given me a book about Greek heroes of antiquity as a birthday present. This Superman of the antique world fascinated me. He could complete the most challenging tasks that average humans couldn't achieve. Already as a child in a crib, he killed with his bare hands two snakes sent by Zeus' jealous spouse Hera, who wished to kill the child of her husband's extramarital affairs. So, Herakles, fathered by a god and given the gift of superhuman strength, was a half-god but shunned by his fellow citizens of the elite at that time. He was good enough to finish the seven superhuman tasks asked of him by various kings, for which he became famous.

I found my quarters comfortable, even a special place for a couple in love, with a comfortable wide bed for two. However, as a poet who pondered his life, wishing a woman to hold and love, he thought about his past muse and to find her last resting place. As a man, he had been a lover of women, and still, some of his fiery libido he once experienced also being felt at times that he still could transfer his love to his present muse to become happy in love, in love between an elderly couple who appreciated each other, and who have become two pals enjoying each other's company. Besides, he was a good team player for realizing some projects initiated by his muse, some minor building improvements to her cottage, and various chores connected with stores around the city.

Although I have been back to the city of art and culture and the first democracy, I see it as the cradle of Western culture, not only because of the heritage of great Classical and Hellenistic art that brought forth Roman culture and, through it, European cultural evolution. Above all, however, when you approach the city, you cannot avoid the view of the Acropolis, which will always be in your viewpoint from wherever you approach the town. If you can afford a cab, you could book ahead on the Internet; you'll travel along poor neighbourhoods and streets filled with many tiny shops and people crowding the streets, cars jam-packed parked on the left and right side, it will need good skills to manoeuvre one's car along one-way streets whose width couldn't take two-way traffic.

As you get closer to the centre of town and experience the five hills of Athens, suddenly, you'll have a first view of the Acropolis. It stands as a symbol not exclusively for art and culture, but one should take the time to read up on the temples of the Parthenon and Erechtheion, the Athena-Nike temple, and the Propylaea. For myself, I see the Parthenon temple first, though the approach my cab driver, Aristos, has taken is to describe to me the five different hills the city is built on and between. It reminds me of the palm of a hand but built on five hills against Rome's seven. I enjoyed this geography lesson as it refreshed the information I had already read about but had laid to rest. We also talk about the economy and touch on politics, but generally, it does not seem vastly different from the remainder of European countries. However, Greece went through more economic hardship than its northern cousins—the Acropolis at a closer look. From now on, as we drive closer to the city, it's the welcome I've expected. The Acropolis appears on the horizon in its might and beauty as we carry along the main streets of Athens. My mind is already thinking about the following tasks I must do for the first time once the driver drops me off at the destination of my temporary apartment at the Airbnb in Markou Botsari Street. Ok, having retrieved the keys from the drop box outside, when the host gave me the code, I entered the apartment at the mezzanine level. I immediately enjoyed the varying lighting levels and the generous bed. The kitchen was brand new, and I quickly adjusted to my shiny new interior.

I opted for the Metro station Syggrou fix and explored the immediate neighbourhood. After entering the Metro, I planned to visit the Plaka, its oldest street, and some of the antiquity monuments, which would take me back to the familiar trails I used to walk many times before, and where many millions of people, visitors, and tourists had tread on before me. How would I feel to walk familiar trails, paths, and streets after so many years since I've visited and lived here? Let's test my senses, let my feet touch the paved ancient roads, and just let me find my trails by an inner sense that'll guide me like a satellite guidance system. But this time, I stepped out of the Metro at Syntagma station, bought a six-day visitor's ticket, and headed back to the Acropoli station. My walk then directed me as if I had been arriving at my second home, noticing the street corners and buildings. I had arrived at a spot that was important to my artistic development. Plaka. The inner city of Athens.

*

Athens Markou Botsari Street

Thursday, February 08.

The cab driver fetched me in the arrival hall, holding a sign with my name. We had to walk a few minutes to where he had parked his car. "I phoned you, but you didn't answer," he said quietly. "I haven't changed my phone from Flight Modus yet," I replied, checking it. I understood that he couldn't drive his cab to the front of the arrival hall due to his contract conditions. I didn't mind, as I haven't paid for that privilege. While he drove me toward Athens, he refreshed my geographical knowledge, naming me the hills of Athens. We travelled through the poorer suburbs, he pointed out to me, and finally, we arrived at my destination. I noticed that I had aged, as I didn't notice immediately the correct entrance to my lodgings. However, after calling the landlady, I found the grey key box near the entrance door. The given code opened the box, and I could retrieve the keys to the apartment on the ground floor.

My first impression: An entrance area in off-white colours, with a massive poster of two white galloping horses covering the two wardrobe doors. White-grey porcelain tiles were placed on the floors. To the left was a kitchenette with an electric stove, sink, washing machine, and floor cupboards, with hung wall cupboards above. Two high cupboards at the end had red lacquered doors, and a free-standing fridge had carmine red doors—a skillful modern interior with a balance of laminates contrasting in white, grey, and cherry reds. At the corner from the anteroom/ wardrobe area is a small round table with a white top, wooden legs, and two matching polyurethane shell chairs. The double bed had a comfortable mattress, white linen, and a dark grey acrylic cover that had been just right for the cool nights. Besides, the air could be warmed by a wall unit, ventilating, cooling, and heating. A double full-height openable glazed door unit behind outdoor Venetian blinds could be used for natural ventilation during warm days. Dark grey curtains could be drawn across the double window units for additional comfort. The flat TV screen had been fixed on the wall opposite the double bed. The well-appointed mini apartment became a modern shell, quite comfortable and compact for a short stay.

Having settled into the chic, modern furnished apartment with pleasing furniture colours, I took my Zeger, locked the door, and walked to the nearby Metro station. I immediately bought a reduced tourist ticket for six days at Syntagma station and had a ride back to Acropoli station.

A First Walk down Vyronos Street

When I emerged on my first day at noon from the Acropoli station, the sense of air and the city noises caught up with my senses that were still reflecting the aftermath of a fine flight from Vienna, the pleasant drive with Aristos, the cab driver from the Taxi Wind Company, which I have booked eight weeks ahead. Crossing over Dionysos Areopagitou into Vyronos Street, I noticed the Vyronos Hotel, where I had lodged together with my spouse on the top floor, which a friend had reserved us inclusive of a sun-flooded balcony, where one had a full view of the north-eastern part of the

Acropolis below a cloudless blue sky. My spouse enjoyed sun tanning while I was doing research at the Public Library.

Further, on the left side, I noticed Demeter, a shop that sells excellent handicraft copies of antiquities as worthwhile souvenirs. Perhaps the man inside the shop must be Giannis, who sold me a handcrafted ceramic box ten years ago. The lid had as a theme kalos eros—the beautiful Eros—painted on it. I have to come back later and talk to him. Further, on the terrace of Lysikratous, at the Café Diogenis, adjacent to the Lysikratous monument, where I used to meet my artist friends and Athina, I took Sellei road opposite Daphne's restaurant to Thespidos, realizing familiar souvenir shops and Brettos, the colourful lit bar.

Babis's ice cream shop is in central Plaka on Kidathineon Street, at 10:00 a.m., a parlour in the existing spot since I came to Athens 24 years ago for the first time. His new assistant, Anna, a fine woman, I bought a yoghurt ice cream from. Babis wasn't in his shop. "Perhaps tomorrow," Anna said. Like many Greeks, Babis joined the adventurers seeking their fortune in the USA to earn a living and acquire capital to open his ice cream shop on his return. His American wife accompanied him and helped him prepare sandwiches in his shop. They made a good team. Babis was talkative and consistently reported on the things that happened most during my absence, and he brought me up to speed on the salient features of his life and local politics.

Around the corner towards the Filom. Eterias Square, the former Café, had been taken over by a new owner who had a crew of renovators working. Just a few metres further, the cafés had changed. The outside sitting area had been glazed with a new roof, providing a contemporary look. The smoked glass attracted tourists looking for a modern restaurant. I missed the old, familiar Island-style atmosphere. I continued down the square and passed the restaurant where my spouse and I had a lobster dinner on our first visit to Athens. A slick waiter who spoke to us as we passed had recommended it and talked us into it. Unfortunately, we both became ill after the meal. I should have never given in to a highly praised seafood specialty. Seafood poisoning is an unpleasant event. Years later, when Athina and her family invited us to this restaurant, as I had told her about our misfortune, she asked the waiter who had talked us into the seafood meal to speak to the owner. The waiter disappeared after he realized my angry looks. She explained to the owner that our bad meal here was making us ill on our first visit to his place. The owner apologized and gave us a special Greek dessert on the house. It still reminded me of the days when I travelled with my spouse. This time, I had taken leave from home and friends. I wished to experience the city compared to my first visit when I had the assistance of Athina, who took me to the north-eastern slope of the Acropolis, the National Archaeological Museum, and an excursion to Delphi, and the temple of Poseidon at Cap Sounion. Although twenty years back, it seemed to have happened only recently, I pondered as I walked the ancient roads and mingled with the crowds, who were not as overpowering a mass as in the summer months.

Athens Panagia Kapnikarea

Yet, as there are no longer tourist seasons, I'm still gladly travelling in the first week of February, when the climate is mild and favourable for walking about the city's trails and streets where most people venture. Tourists prefer direct routes to visit the sites of antiquity. However, changing my routes slightly with some side streets in the same direction renders empty streets away from the trodden path of mass tourism, like Adrianou Street, the main street in Plaka and the oldest street in Athens. Then, right into Kekropos Street and Thoukididou corner Imperidou and Vouilis Street, passed Elektra Metropolis Athens into Mitropoleos Street, crossing Filellinon Street to Syntagma Square. I buy a padded envelope at the post office and walk along Filellinon Street to the end of the northwest area of Syntagma Square. Using my six-day ticket, I travel back and forth between the Airbnb and the city. As I emerge at the Metro station Syggrou Fix, I cross Leoforos, Andrea Syggrou, and Kallirois into Markou Botsari Street off Despos Sechou Street, where I enter my Airbnb and relax. Along Kallirois at a small grocery shop, I bought a box of Tourokopita pastry and warmed it in the oven. Delicious. I have to use the time switch for the shower for hot water and enjoy the shower. I dry off and put on my easy gear, eat the warmed-up food, and continue with my notes. Reading a bit, I doze off in the generous bed to the music on Kosmos TV. I wake up and dress to continue my walk through the city.

It was my first trip from Kynosargous to the city, only two subway stops from Syggrou Fix, a short walk from my accommodation, which I had good luck finding on the Internet. I continued on foot from the Syntagma station, emerging from the subway and crossing Syntagma Square on a slight downslope, paved with stone slabs forming a pattern, towards Ermou Street, lying on an axis, renovated for the Olympic Games in 2014. Well-appointed stores for fashion and luxury department stores line this impressive mall; towards its middle, one sees the Panagia Kapnikarea, one of the oldest Byzantine churches of Athens, well positioned at Ermou Street's axis, with the streets around shaping the Plateía Kapnikarea, the Square, where once a temple stood for honouring the goddess, Athena. On those bases, the Byzantine church was built in the 12th century. I followed the familiar street connecting Syntagma Square with Monastiraki Square. I walked around Panagia Kapnikarea admiring its architecture and recalled having lit a candle on my last visit to Ana-Anetha.

I continued on Kapnikarea Street and passed the Hotel Acropolis, where I stayed with my spouse during our first visit to Athens, toward Adrianou Street. I passed Agora Square and turned left onto Adrianou Street. The street, which hasn't been changed since antiquity, is known for its souvenirs, fashion, and jewellery shops. I noticed a shop for upmarket watches that had not changed its position in twenty years. But this time, although I felt familiar vibes, the scene offered me a different perspective from the days I had been for the first time in Athens, meeting a muse. The ebb and flow of time had polished the memory of my muse to become a perfectly smooth pebble on the beach of Monemvassia.

Athens Kapnikareas Street with a view of the Acropolis

Still, my perspective on the art and the places of antiquity had increased in the splendour of their appearance. My feet followed a radar of awareness of memory to reach the Plaka's heart along Kidathineion Street.

I passed Babis's shop again and remembered his friendly attitude when I entered it ten years ago. He chatted with me about the latest news in his city and the country. Since then, whenever I came to his ice cream shop, he would welcome me like a lost friend and chat with me, carrying on our discussion from the last visit. Over the years, we became good friends, and my first visit, whenever I came to Athens, was to Babis's ice cream shop at Plaka. This time, I did not find him in his shop, and I missed his lively report and comment on the current state of his health, the city, and the nation. But perhaps tomorrow. I enjoyed walking these familiar roads, even If I crisscrossed them once or twice.

I walked back to Adrianou Street, down to Lysistratous, turned to the right, and approached the Lysistratous monument, where Lord Byron wrote his famous poem, *The Childe Herold.* Behind the excavations is a café with a terrace, where I met my muse at the turn of the 21st century, talking poetry. Down Vyronos Road toward Dionysou Areopagitou, I saw the dark green sign of Demeter, a fine shop for hand-painted pottery, copies of classical Greek vases and boxes, figures and busts, where I bought my first box for keeping personal items. The shop survived due to the excellent products it offered. I entered and admired the hand-made ceramic pieces. I spoke to the salesman, Giannis, and he told me the same old story: "These products are all hand-made ceramic pieces, based on examples of antiquity, made by the daughter of the brother of the dictator Papadopoulos." I agreed with a nod. "Yes, I recall having bought a small ceramic box with a lid many years ago depicting 'Kalos Eros.'" He looked me over for a moment. "Yes," he mumbled, "we had those 10-15 years back." I was as much stunned as he was, thinking back. I feared how fast time had passed and our memories had faded. However, this box, in black and burnt clay colours, lives on my bookshelf near my desk. It had survived the trips from Athens to Johannesburg, then back to Athens and again to Vienna, a roundtrip of half the earth's longitude. Indeed. I saw the joy on his face that I appreciated his artistic copies of Greek Classical artefacts.

Across Dionysou Areopagitou, I entered the metro station Akropoli, travelled for one stop, and emerged at Syntagma Square. A heavy police presence controlled a student demonstration. I walked across the Square and down memory lane in thought: Ermou Street, the small artistic fountain, and the shops for fashion and jewellery on both sides. I missed the paper and stationery shop, which was a must-visit with excellent offers. Already halfway down from Syntagma Square, the Byzantine church Panagia Kapnikareia will be visible; its dominant cupola with red clay tiles and its light sand-coloured tones in the stone is most pleasant to the eye. Its proportions change as one comes closer, but they will always be in a well-balanced composition of its parts. The blue-grey pallid skies and the darker grey of the square basalt paving stones of the street framed the view of the church and enhanced the stone to become a honey-yellow colour. The entrance door was locked today, so I couldn't light a candle for my muse.

Turning left into Kapnikareia Street, I passed the Hotel Acropolis and continued toward Café Idria on Adrianou Street, opposite Plateia Agoras. However, renovation work at the café prevented me from sitting down for a cup of coffee at the corner table where Ana-Anetha and I met for a first chat, and I experienced the same attraction as over the medium of the Internet and the telephone. Immediately, that scene sprung to mind, and even our conversation sounded coming alive. I continued toward the eastern end of the area around the Hadrian's Library, where I turned left into Aiolou Street, the monument of the Tower of the Winds, the Horologion of Andronikos Cyrrhestes, an ancient tower indicating weather and time. Recalling our first walk toward the Acropolis, we spent time musing about the buildings opposite, a small width of one room facing west, on Mark. Avriliou Street, with an entrance door a few steps up, framed by a bougainvillea bush, and a window with a wrought iron protective grill in a Classical geometrical pattern. A pair of French windows led to a balcony on the first floor. The sand-coloured walls with horizontally ruled groves at 30 cm intervals reminded me of the Classicistic building period. White bands were painted around window openings, cornices, and decorative elements. "This is where I imagine writing my novel about the Acropolis," I told Ana-Anetha. She seemed to enjoy my short fantasy trip and smiled. "Well, I assume your study is on the first floor, where you certainly have a great view of these places of antiquity, inspiring you."

I walked back to Adrianou Street and headed for Filomousou Eterias Square, turning left into Kidathineion Street, then right into Farmáki Street, and visiting the Trattoria Pizzeria. It had changed, modernized, streamlined outdoor gazebos with lots of stained glass. It had lost its original atmosphere due to its sparse appearance, which had blended well with the buildings of the Square of the old days. This was our usual haunt when my spouse and I visited Athens; the old owner was present, greeting us, and the two waiters, one bent slightly backward when serving, while the other bent slightly forward, an amusing picture, were gone with the old interior. However, I sat at a window table and enjoyed some traditional kleftiko while the waiter pointed out the old man's son to me. He spoke fluent English while the new owner bowed his head slightly.

I returned to Syntagma Square and checked out the 'Public' Store and its coffee shop on the top floor, which overlooks Syntagma Square and the parliament building. I ordered an espresso and sipped the refreshing drink. Ana-Anetha discussed some recent historical events with me when she used to teach literature at a secondary school in Athens. I felt I had enough for the first day revisiting Athens, so I headed to the lift, exited at ground floor level, crossed the square, passed the refreshing fountain, and entered the metro by walking down the stairs. Two stations later, I emerged at Syggrou Fix. Crossing both one-way lanes of Kallirrois Street, I entered the small supermarket next to the Petrol Station for some groceries. Then, the steeper road, Markou Botsari Street, is always an uphill walk to my rented temporary apartment, the luxury Airbnb. I made coffee and a sandwich and enjoyed the food. Meanwhile, sitting at the round table in a shell seat, I observed the shiny cherry red cupboards of the kitchenette, with its pristine white working surfaces and appliances, save for the big fridge in cherry red. Then, I went to bed, watched TV, enjoyed the music on a radio channel, and fell asleep. I had arrived in Athens.

I recall waking in the middle of the night, having dreamt about Angels and Demons, Ana-Athina as a priestess at the Nike temple, and her sudden appearance from the seventh column of the Parthenon. Then I was falling and felt the sensation of tumbling into the sea at Sounion, a white ship with dark-blue sails passing, with a portrait of Athina on its main sail. Would she save me from drowning?

Friday, February 09.

It is an excellent, warm morning for February. I showered, dressed, made breakfast, ate and enjoyed my oats and fruit, washed my dishes, took my Zeger, and headed downhill towards the metro station Syggrou Fix. I emerged at Akropoli station and headed for the Plaka, passing the Tower of Winds, where my memory kicked in, recalling the walk with my muse at the turn of the century. The ascent through existing roads toward the Acropolis had changed in character as more domiciles had been refurbished and newly built in twenty years. The small path originally became a tarred road next to the fence of the Acropolis area. New, well-designed domiciles have blocked the view over Athens on a premier site. Soon, I reached the area around the ticket office and was offered a reduced ticket for foreign visitors at a discount, usual for the Pre-spring season. There were two people before me attaining tickets. My mobile phone was on standby; I was alerted by the crystal-clean air and the rising sun to take many photographs. The morning light was perfect; with the sun rising, I accessed the Propylaea and worked the high steps up, noticing the renovation works on the Nike temple with the sun rays radiating the marble columns. Passed the Propylaea, where wooden floor planks facilitated the uneven walk, the way towards the Parthenon had been paved with precast concrete floor slabs to overcome the natural, uneven, rocky ground formation. The rocks have been polished by the millions of feet walking across for about 100 years, often slipping even with sneakers or athletic shoes. The walking is now resolved for everybody's comfort and safety, concentrating on the vistas more pleasantly.

The Parthenon's west gable, where I had dreamt that Ana-Anetha had emerged the other night. She appeared seamlessly from the seventh column, an apparition, but at the same time tactile and natural. I took my snapshots of memorable vistas of details of the pediment, especially a photograph of the north-western corner with some remains of the sculptures, their originals removed and placed in the New Acropolis Museum (NAM). At the same time, some casts had been replaced, probably an Attic reclining hero. The Doric-Peripteral temple, made from Pentelic marble, was designed by Iktinos and Kallikrates.

Athens Café Ydria Adrianou Street

Pericles entrusted Pheidias with the supervision. The temple has no straight lines starting on its base and has a convex curvature towards the middle, contained in the whole construction of the temple and its façade. This allowed a rectilinear effect and worked against a negative optical illusion that would have been created if cold horizontal lines had been employed. Besides, the columns have been worked with an entasis, a gradual reduction from the middle upwards. The columns were placed with an incline towards the temple's centre, beside the thickening corner columns. Further column spaces were reduced slightly toward the corners, and the metopes' size decreased gradually from the centre to the edges of the frieze. Technical and aesthetical considerations combined resulted in a Classical masterpiece in the development of the Greek temple. Quite a development to be appreciated on this Parthenon III temple. The first one, an archaic Doric temple built in the 6th century BC from limestone, the 'Hekatompedon', as it was 100 ancient attic feet long, as known from literary sources and inscriptions. The few surviving elements and sculptures can be seen in the Acropolis Museum. After the fall of the tyrants in Athens, Parthenon II was probably built after the battle of Marathon (490 BC). The Persians burned the temple down in 480 BC, and also other monuments. The construction of the Parthenon III began in 447 BC on the same site as the destroyed Parthenon II, dedicated to Athena Parthenos, and finished in 432 BC, designed by the architects Iktinos and Kallikrates, who were also responsible for its construction.

Project Management was in the hands of Pheidias, Pericles's friend and counsellor in all cultural undertakings.

The Parthenon is a Doric-Peripteral temple with eight columns on each gable façade and seventeen on its long sides. The column ratio of 8 x 17 is an exception to the Doric temple design of this period, which featured 8 x 13 columns. The temple's foundations, on a slight curvature, were taken over from Parthenon II and extended to the build-up of the whole temple. Besides, the building was extended to the north. On this curved krepidoma, the temple walls rest on, the gable facades and long sides surrounded by the tall and dominant Doric colonnade. By using the curved line of the krepidoma, the architects avoided the effects of a negative optic illusion that would have happened if accurate vertical lines of the base (krepidoma) had been employed. Furthermore, the columns had been carved with an entasis, gradually reducing their thickness from their middle upwards; the incline of the columns toward the centre on the gable facades (pteron); the thickening of the four corner columns; the reduction of the column spaces of the corner columns; the gradual decrease of the metopes from the centre to the edges of the frieze. These technical adjustments also complement the aesthetical design of the architects.

The third vertical division of the temple, besides the krepidoma and colonnade, the entablature, consists of the epistyle, the frieze (metopes and triglyphs), and the cornice. Together with the pediments, this division represents the culmination of the entire architectural composition and shows the master design of Pheidias. One arrives at the pronaos, representing the temple's cella entrance with six slender Doric columns. From the pronaos, one enters the temple's cella, which is 30 metres long (approximately 100 ancient Attic feet, hence the cella's epithet of 'Hekatompedon'). The cult statue of the goddess Athena stood here. Two superposed Doric colonnades of ten columns each divide the space and its width into three naves. A third, smaller colonnade, superposed with square pilasters at its corners, linked the two others behind the statue's base. It formed an elongated plan with arms extended to the east and terminating at shafts attached to the wall.

The back of the central area surrounded by the colonnades was reserved for the chryselephantine statue of Athena Parthenos, Pheidias's master plan. Today, fragments of the pedestal and the hole at its centre to receive the shaft of the statue's frame can be seen. The statue was made of gold and ivory. Gold was used for the goddess's raiment, while ivory was reserved for exposed body parts. These materials were fitted to the internal wooden skeletal structure. The gold parts weighed over a ton, could be easily removed, and their weight checked. The statue, an impressive work of their time, was 12 metres tall. It had been lost in the 5th century AD, apparently moved by Christians to Constantirople. This statue is known today through marble copies of the Roman period (see National Archaeological Museum). It is also known from Pausanias, who saw it in situ in the 2rd century BC. According to his description, the goddess was standing, armed, and richly decorated on a high pedestal adorned with a relief frieze, representing the birth of Pandora. The goddess held a Nike in her right hand while her left hand rested on her shield.

Walking around the Parthenon temple, I observed the extensive and careful renovations. The sun rose between the eastern columns, and the shadows on the building and rocky ground were tinted blue, matching the light blue-grey strip of the distant mountain range. Light streams and flashes through the hypostyle hall, turning the temple into a light-flooded sculpture. The great temple started to hum, and the maidens from the Erechtheion on the opposite side, warmed up by the rising sun, had intonated a chorus in this musical dialogue. I recalled a concert by Pink Floyd when the lead singer started his lyrical presentation, and the chorus of female singers started their musical dialogue amidst a white smoke rising like fog that became absorbed by sunlight sculpting the outlines of the participants. Although I achieved the ascent and walked about with some difficulty for two hours, the spirit of the place lifted my own. The atmosphere around the Parthenon temple made me forget my tired feet, and after a walk around the temple, I visited the Erechtheion dominating the north side of the Acropolis. Its name is related to Erechtheus, a mythical king of Athens. The Erechtheion represents unique peculiarities, externally and in the arrangement of areas and levels of the cella. The temple's cella on the east side resembles a regular prostyle Ionic temple, with six columns measuring 6,59 metres.

Athens Agora Tower of Winds

The northernmost column of this elevation is in the British Museum. The floor on the west side of the temple is three metres below the floor on the east side. The north porch is lower than the south porch and provides the temple's west part entrance. The tomb of Erechtheus was located in the porch area. The porch of the Caryatids is situated on the south side of the temple in a position related to the north porch. This porch has a parapet on which the six Korae stand and support the entablature and the roof. On the parapet's east side, a small stair leads to the tomb and altar of Kekrops, located on the south side of the Erechtheion. The cella, opposite the Ionic porch, was dedicated to the worship of Athena Polias, the city's defender, and contained her cult statue made of olive wood, to which the Arrephoroi offered the gold-woven peplos during the Panathenaic procession. In front of her statue, a wick burnt in a golden lamp, designed by the sculptor Kallimachos. Next to it was a tall bronze palm tree, which, according to Pausanias, absorbed the smoke. The western portion of the cella had a tripartite division three metres lower than the eastern one. In its eastern section, the part of the west had two small chambers with entrances leading to the prothalamos, or entrance chamber, access to which had been provided by the gates of the north porch. The prothalamos, with the small opening on the south side, communicated with the Porch of the Caryatids. This part of the temple was devoted to the veneration of Poseidon-Erechtheus, and apart from the altar of Poseidon, there were also altars of Boutes and Hephaistos. This was also the home of oikouros ophis, or domiciled serpent of the

Acropolis, a chthonic worship originally represented by Erechtheus or Erechthonios. Athena had a direct relationship with this snake, also depicted near the spear of her chryselephantine statue in the Parthenon. According to tradition, it was at this point that Poseidon hit the rock with his trident during the contest with Athena, thus causing sea water to gush forth. Pausanias calls this the 'well,' and it was located below the floor of the antechamber. Pediment roofs covered the cella entablature and the north porch. The latter roof was lower, and its axis was vertical to the cella roof. The Porch of the Caryatids, with its entablature, had a flat roof. The shape and architectural peculiarities, both internal and external, were conceived by the architect Philokles and dealt with the morphology of the ground and the height differences between the levels. It conserved the holy traces on the site and offered solutions for the needs of worship transferred from the 'ancient temple' to the new building. The Erechtheion is ornate, light, and fresh, distinguishable for its architectural details and sculptural decorations that have been depicted with sensitivity and refinement. The frieze of the cella and the north wall was an incredibly artistic feature. Blue Eleusian marble plaques supported the figures of the frieze made from Paros marble. Their subject connected to the mythical figures of Ion, Kekrops, Erechtheus, and Eumolpos. The corners of the pediments had marble acroteria, while the sima was decorated with lion heads. The temple's highlight is the Porch of the Caryatids (Maidens) on its south porch, which dominates the surrounding area with grace and beauty. Five of the original Caryatids are exhibited in the

Acropolis Museum, while the sixth, removed by Lord Elgin, is in the British Museum.

Prerequisites for these most outstanding masterpieces in architecture, sculpture, and art were based on the new mindset embodied by Pericles, who led Athens to its unique cultural climax, as chairman of the building committee, oversaw the overall planning of the Acropolis, with excellent builders, architects, and sculptors, like Pheidias, Iktinos, and Kallikrates.

The dominant trilogy of the Propylaea, Parthenon, and Erechtheion rises on the broad Acropolis plateau. From the point of composition, there might be no relationship between these buildings. Still, Archaeologists see an inner, hidden relationship that might not be obvious to us. Gottfried Gruben saw the Propylaea (celebratory festival gate), the Erechtheion (effortless grace), and the Parthenon (dignity and majestic size) as a celebratory triad.

Back to the highest point and the lover's leap, where I recalled thoughts about suicide as Athina became ill with terminal cancer. I had to move on, but an emotional uproar still roamed through my soul to get on with enjoying this beautiful morning on the 'Sacred Rock', enriched through an enormously rich history, a sacred ground for prayer and love. It was also the place for death for many Athenians during the occupation by external forces and barbaric riots of warlords. Down again through the impressive Propylaea, enjoying the Nike temple on the left side and further down the steps, 'The Stones of Athens,' the pebble-type assembly of flat-roofed houses and buildings in the near distance.

Downhill toward the Plaka is now different. The paved and tarred road sections that lead to newly built houses bring me toward the Byzantine Chapel of Metamorphosis, where Athina took me for offering our souls to the spirit that had ruled above us and, as she thought, had brought us together in 2000 and, for another visit in 2002. Down steep streets and paths, I arrived again at the Tower of Winds and Adrianou Street.

Carrying on to visit the Byzantine Church of Georgio Epikoos, where I met Athina one evening for a tête-à-tête, an aerobic encounter standing against the south façade's wooden door facing the Cathedral of Mitropoleos. Many tourists mingled here, and I met a woman from Australia who asked me about the symbolic sculptures on the eastern façade of the ancient church. "It's about pagan symbols fending off the bad spirits, as I see it," I told her and added, "but you'll find a detailed explanation online.

Musings by the poet at the Agora of Athens on his second day visiting Monastiraki.

It might have been by accident that I tumbled into the jewellery shop at the Flea Market at Monastiraki. I travelled by Metro to Syntagma Square and then walked along Ermou Street, a favourite street of mine, toward the ancient Byzantine Church, passed the water fountain crossing Mikis Street and Voulis Street, passed fancy designer boutiques, world-label fashion, and upmarket warehouses toward Panagia Kapnikarea (Holy University Church of the Presentation of the Virgin Mary), a Greek Orthodox Church from the 11th century with beautiful ancient frescoes. It's visible from afar, a town planning jewel appreciated in contrast to the soulless modernist buildings surrounding it. I walk around its southeast façade into Kapnikareas Street, the first street I recall I had a great revelation about as I observed the poetess Ana Anetha, Athina, walking along it towards me for a face-to-face meeting dressed in a charcoal woollen coat and loose dark hair. She walked with a controlled, steady gait. I waited near the small Pandrossou market, greeted each other like old friends, and we wouldn't give way to our free emotions, as she was afraid that someone she knew could observe her meeting me. We entered the Café Ydria and exchanged our first impressions of our meeting. Today, twenty years later, the café is still in business being renovated for the summer season.

At the end of Pandrossou Street, I notice Aiolou Street, and at the edge southeast of the Roman Agora with a view of the Klepsydra, I walk along Lisiou Street around the Roman Agora to Polignotou Street and turn right to Dioskurou Street to Pikitis and right into Aeros Street walking toward Monastiraki Square. Through the flea market, I get to Kinetou Street to the left and, at the start of Adrianou Street, to the entrance of Agora's ticket office. The friendly woman at the kiosk surprises me with a reduced ticket to the standard price. "In winter, half price for foreign visitors," she said and smiled. That is very social and will entice the poet to return quickly. The Agora has a vibrant history that still talks to sensitive and receptive visitors. For me, it always has been an area of antiquity where one is faced with the fantastic reconstruction of the Stoa of Attalos, where one has an opportunity, especially on rainy or clouded days, to amble with a friend and discuss critical personal issues or meeting a sweetheart and enjoy exchanges of thoughts. At the same time, one uses walking together to clear up one's mind. But this time, I had no friends, not even from the past, who came along to amble with at the Stoa of Attalos. And neither were they polite to spare some of their time for me. I guess I have been written off as a friend, more as an old man, as the Viennese dialect puts it: *Geh' Oida.*

I read the inscriptions on the destroyed walls, the foundation walls, and the destroyed walls of the various buildings. Enjoy the leisurely walk along the pathways connecting the different structures of antiquity or what had been left by the destruction of the Barbarians. I arrived at the Middle Agora, where I paused and chose a low marble block warmed up by the pre-spring sun to sit on. My mind jumped about, and I recalled Odysseas Elytis' writings. It was a special moment for me as I experienced the Agora's tranquillity and the Acropolis's nearness. When I looked up, I could see the northern slope of the Sacred Rock with the Erechtheion and the Parthenon.

When Odysseas Elytis wrote about moments of immense innerness, I could at this sun-filled morning experience in my conscious world where my subconscious reality was experienced by me, as if I was high up in the pre-spring air of Athens looking down on this lonely poet who undertook to put his inner voice of bearing, where his imagination had suddenly become a stark reality, just like the physical world I have been walking through for the last three days. It goes back much further than that, but I have noticed this in such an inner shook-up state of peace and tranquillity that my thinking had become sharp and clear. And I wrote: Like Odysseas Elytis, the poet experienced the writings of Andreas Embeirikos as a robust prompt for his expression of Eros, as Sam Hamill refers to in his Prolog of Olga Broumas's translation of *Selected and Last Poems of Odysseas Elytis* in *Eros, Eros, Eros*. This poet had been introduced to the great Greek poets through Ana-Anetha-Athina Thanou, herself a poetess and writer and a friend of the poet.

This happening had been the poet's first great revelation in understanding modern poetry. The second revelation was the great love the poet found as he fell in love with the poetess, who asked: "For which genre of poetry do you aim and what kind of poet would you like to be known for?" He didn't have to think about it, as it had been clear to him: "The Poet of Love" was his immediate answer. Athina just gazed at him. Since then, the poet has found his voice in erotic poetry. In this regard, he had experienced Odysseas Elytis for himself as a leading poet, and he immediately related to him, even if he had at first not yet fully grasped the depth of his voice.

The third revelation had been his visit to the temporary grave of the poetess Athina Thanos. At first, it was a tragedy for the love of his life, an unsurmountable fate the poet wrestled with for many years until he could write poetry and prose about love. It had been such a mind opener for the poet who then, as he stood at her temporary gravesite, had a shaking emotional experience realizing the depth of his love for her. Her death not only rattled his innermost, but it had changed his life forever.

*

INTERMEZZO: Recalling memory flashes of Waterfield cottage and its surroundings.

Waterfield—Viennese Walking Trail Number nine passes the Waterfield section, where I stay temporarily until winter sets in, temperatures drop below zero, and the cottage cools down too much. I get up at 6 a.m., prepare breakfast, don my Nordic walking outfit, lock the cottage, and take my trusted Nordic walking sticks. I sometimes take my rucksack with a water bottle and a short-sleeved tee shirt for longer walks, and I'm on my way. In about five minutes, I reach the South tangent of the city motorway and pass it below to join again walking trail No.9. It leads along endless greens, shrubs, and cops of trees on its right side, a denser wooded area on the left up to the 'Lusthaus' established 1876 on these former hunting grounds of the Kaiser. It's my first time undertaking this Nordic walking tour, as all first undertakings are still cumbersome. I had a one-year problem-solving time to stay healthy, which led to the detection of kidney stones. Fortunately, the problem had been detected at my usual Andrologist, but as it had not been seen clearly on the ultrasound device, I had to visit a C.T. scan in Stockerau, which made it clear. I had to be operated on, but at first, a stent had to be inserted into the urethral canal to protect the kidney. All went well, but having no car meant a lot of effort for me to reach the specialists' surgeries on time. Mrs Ina helped me to get some relief by chauffeuring me to a doctor and specialist. Having been given an operating date in two months, I looked forward to leading a healthy life again. Dr Ghazil, an experienced female surgeon, operated. I was well again after a four-day stay in the hospital LK KOR, as named for short. I knew this hospital from the operation on my hip joints and one knee joint. What would I have done without Mrs Ina? She could help me immediately after I had a night-long colic attack. A nearby surgery known to her helped me with a urine test and some antibiotic pills before my Androl-ogist opened her surgery and sent me to a C.T. scan.

All these thoughts still circulate in my mind as I walk and rely on my exercises to get fit again. At the age of 84, I'm still determined to stay healthy, and I'm motivated by Mrs Ina, who adheres to her exercise program of swimming regularly. Although I have to accommodate my literary interests in writing and drawing, the continuing dialogue of artistic un-dertaking has fascinated me from an early age. But it's es-sential to stay healthy, as I still have many tasks ahead of me. It's always a particular morning when Ina comes around from her early morning swim nearby. Having just arrived from my early morning walk, I prepare a pot of Earl Grey tea. I use the Nordic walking sticks to keep my back posture straight and propel me forward. It's a great feeling, as I ha-ven't done this for a year. It disciplines me and corrects my tired posture that has suffered so much this year, 2024.

I will exercise and reach a fitness level to enter 2025 with renewed energy. My thoughts clear up, and I see myself between a spouse of 80 and a lady friend of 85. Well, I'm a happy man who receives attention from my spouse at times, who keeps up with the news and the cultural happenings, reads the leading papers, and who reminds me of worthwhile articles about the tragic love of two artists, Christine Levant, and Werner Berg, I've never would have come across but for my spouse. For ten years, we have fought for an adequate existence in an impossible bedsitter for two artists: B, the idea-forging spout in fashion design she modelled on herself, and Z, the artist and poet who emerged from his architectural profession. While his client list dried out continuously, he resorted to odd jobs with his engineer friend Carl, and they did some excellent work together, though not that spectacularly grand.

While funds diminished quickly, my spouse and I decided to sell our renovated cottage and move on to Greece for an interlude. I hoped that as Z, the artist, I could impress the art-loving Greeks with my innovative paintings and achieve some sales. I had been entirely wrong regarding the selling aspect, while the paintings and drawings seemed to generate good interest, albeit mainly with the younger crowd of visitors. A deep recession clouded our happy years there. Finally, we had to move on to Austria. B had the arduous task of selling our life's collection of linen, furniture, artworks, artifacts, and my library of close to 1000 books, besides all the canvases I had painted over three years, for a pittance. Fortunately, I could save my 14 canvases of the Apollo frieze, which I had successfully exhibited at EPASKT-Gallery in Plaka. However, the market for contemporary art was dormant and depressed. Nobody bought first-class, well-looked-after furniture, but a teacher bought my whole library for a nominal amount, so my spouse had some survival money. B was heartbroken; we couldn't afford to stay in Greece longer, as we had to service our new accommodation in Klnbg-Weidling. Our lives had been turned upside down. Original Greek friends at our accommodation turned out to be no friends, save for the husband of the landlady and one visiting friend—two genuine human beings. I honour them: Nefelis and Mr Gregory. I had failed my spouse, my landlord, and my artistic efforts.

We arrived at the centre for repatriation in Vienna. It was a shameful way to be treated as an Austrian citizen who had terrible luck being economically thrown out of his profession and whose capital from the sale of his houses had to save them both from falling into the gutter of an African township. Damned! My spouse was ill and had to recover, but she still shared with me the hardship of rebuilding a shattered life, even if so meagre and not adequate for an architect who couldn't find work in the capital of Austria to support himself and his wife. One Sunday afternoon, we both wandered into the shop Art Forum. Thank God, we thought we had finally found friendly and compassionate people.

Falling in love is easy. Like most people, I fell in love many times, but writing about love meant having at least experienced the most basic types of love: agape, instant head-over-heels love, passionate sexual love, erotic love, and compassionate love. Most of the time, especially in my young, growing years, I craved sexual love; we all do. Would we be here otherwise? Agape: The poet experiences at least two women who have decided to stay away from the fires of passion that not only burn but could kill. Indeed. I often think of Ana, Anetha, and AKA Athina. How would our relationship have carried on, what avenue would a passionate love affair have taken, and when would that lava of an intense inner burn have ceased? To what level of intensity could even passionate love rise? Athina always mentioned the tale of a Chinese Emperor who never could get enough of sexual love encounters until he died of exhaustion, having loved to death. Does that mean that passionate love will ultimately lead to the death of star-struck lovers? Is it why she asked me: *Is love death?* Thinking about it 20 years later, I have to agree with her. She had given me a most precious present: Years of sexual love starting with agape, continuing with cyber love, and ending with physical love of star-struck lovers; that in itself is a lottery win. She smiled when we fitted like a hand in glove and complemented each other like nobody else in her and my experience.

I think about Ina, the name I've given her, which suits her personality. She came into my life when I couldn't stand my spouse of 34 years, suddenly having continuous fights and misunderstandings. I always wondered what Athina thought of her when she met her and invited us for dinner. Probably, we could all become good friends, but then love, this fickle spirit, jumped into the person of Athina, remaining in her before her untimely death due to a terminal illness.

It seemed to be the end of an unusually intense relationship.

At first, I suffered from interrupted sleep and a lack of concentration in my work as a freelance architect. Then, as work ran out, I turned to poetry and drawing to express my feelings.

My friend Carl, the structural engineer I worked with on my building alterations and extensions, used to take me out and cheer me up while my spouse had to deal with her own health problems. We couldn't help each other during last year's stay in Afrique du Sud.

In 2009, we renovated our cottage and pool, refurbished the kitchen, and rearranged the front garden. Then, looking for an agent, we found someone with good connections in the realty business. He decided to take our property under his wing and find a genuine buyer who would afford the price we agreed upon.

Waiting for two months was tiring, as we had to sit in a café on Sundays when prospective buyers would visit our cottage.

As my study was annexed to the main building, it caught the eye of a couple, both teachers, who became the new owners of our property. Our cottage reminded them of their parents' accommodation in the countryside.

Athens Acropolis Parthenon Corner detail

Damned! Athina had suffered an unpleasant and horrible death while I thought about suicide. Indeed. Unbearable at first, whenever we met, we loved as love came to us, naturally, like breathing. We felt like one body, one mind, and one soul. It was an incredible experience, but also it could have meant my death when she passed on. However, I still felt responsible for my spouse, but it dawned on me that this wasn't just a casual love affair. It had gone so deep that Athina spoke of marriage, kids, and life together if we had met earlier. Probably, we would have been married with children. I often felt like that, too, but even if we gave each other that gift, it could no longer happen. This, my friends and muses, was a perfect love too late for a lifetime and establishing a family, but it would have been. Was it another Greek tragedy? Indeed. I have felt it physically and mentally and, since then, have written about it in poetry, short stories, memoirs, and thrillers. Athina and her love have inspired me. I sincerely thank her. Ina felt that way, too, as I fell in love with her. She said: "We both had our great love experiences," and she offered me friendship. Something I have experienced with my spouse, but then we had once madly loved. Since Ina and I have experienced being a good team together, we have completed some projects successfully, starting with her initiative. Besides, we like to spend time together and discuss topics ranging from daily events to art and literature. This is agape, I think, but even a bit more with a strain of eroticism blended in now and then between us. At times, I had dreams of seducing her, yet I respect the spouse of a friend.

Often, I noticed her husband is jealous, although no longer virile, but despite it. He dislikes me for that aspect and continuously asks me about it. I have stopped answering. Ina deserves her own life and space; I respect her for that. That's why we continue to be good friends. Her hubby feels that and terrorizes her, demanding to be taken here and there in the city, as she is an excellent driver. I gave her a Roman First to park her car in the tightest parking lots in Vienna, and I was her friend, guide, and accompanying partner since she offered me the bands of friendship.

*

Back to the city of Athens.

I entered the 'Public' warehouse at Syntagma Square and requested the Department of Literature. On the second floor, the saleslady showed me the shelf with Odysseas Elytis's translations of poetry in English. I knew those offered but expected new translations from his oeuvre. Then I remembered Athina's words: "Better get them from USA publishers." I did when I still lived in South Africa. The universities have excellent scholars versed in Greek and English, so editions are magnificent. I found a book by Samarakis and took it to the cashier, but there was a change of shifts. I waited 10 minutes and then asked a saleslady if I could pay my six euros for the book, but she didn't take my money, so I left. Amazing. I zig-zagged the streets back to Plaka and wanted to see if Babis had arrived at his ice cream shop. It was closed, although Anna had said yesterday that he would be here today. I was disappointed.

Athens Acropolis Parthenon East corner elevation

I haven't seen Babis for 14 years. Instead, I browsed some souvenir shops for pins I collected to attach to my beret and caps. I discovered three. I bought them in two shops: Alexander the Great's head, the Phaistos disc, and Leonidas' 'molon lave' ('come and get it'). Sparta's king told the invading Persians at the Thermopylae. Then, I bought a bronze owl used as a paperweight in another shop, recalling that Ina had numerous accounts to consolidate and be weighted down.

The time was right to visit the New Acropolis Museum for the umpteenth time. I have loved this museum since its opening. Masses of people were roaming about, and I managed only two floors: the ground floor, which houses the findings from sanctuaries and settlements that developed on the slopes of the Acropolis throughout all historical periods, and the first floor, which contains the entire history on the summit of the Rock, from the second millennium BC to the end of antiquity.

By then, I had run out of steam, and the amassing of tourists tired me. I became thirsty. I walked to the nearby Metro station, Acropoli, and headed to my temporary home at Kynosargous on Markou Botsari Street. Next to the metro station, Syggrou Fix, opposite the one-way traffic, I entered my favourite small food store that keeps fruit, fast food to prepare, and ice cream. I bought Spinakopita, some bread, and some ice cream. Walking uphill at Markou Botsari Street is beneficial for walking around central Athens and is an excellent visual experience. I took a hot shower and went to bed for an hour. Then I prepared my dinner and wrote my journal.

SATURDAY 10.02.

I bought a selection of fruit at a nearby fruit shop. The oranges are sweet this time of year, the lemons are juicy, the tomatoes have a mildly sweet taste, and the olives taste tangy. I talked with the man from Bangladesh and was amazed that he even weighed my shopping bag. But what for? He didn't answer my question. I took my purchase home and prepared my Zeger to leave for the city centre. The effective subway took me to Acropoli station, and I hurried to the Acropolis Museum. A few people were at the ticket hall at 9:30 in the morning, and my visit was enjoyable.

I immediately took the lift to the third floor, which presented the sculptural decoration of the Parthenon. This space is designed as a glass-walled chamber that wraps around a rectangular core whose orientation and dimensions match those of the Parthenon's original cella.

The outer walls of the core incorporate the relief-carved blocks of the temple's Ionic frieze, mounted in the same position as they were on the monument but at a lower height for better viewing. The Metopes are hung in pairs between the steel columns of the hall with the same numbers as the Parthenon columns. The colossal figures of the two pediments have been mounted on low pedestals at the east and west sides of the gallery, where they are visible from all directions.

The exhibition combines the original marble sculptures with plaster copies of those retained in the British Museum or other foreign museums. The glass walls enclosing the gallery provide natural lighting and allow a direct line of sight between the sculptures and the monument from which they come.

In the atrium and vestibule of the Parthenon Gallery, additional information is offered concerning the gold and ivory statue of Athena Parthenos, the operation of the Acropolis sanctuary, and the political situation in the city when the grand building was built. I was lost in thought admiring the Frieze and walked a few times around the core as well, always finding a new angle to look at these masterpieces of Classical art. Time had passed quickly. I finally freshened up my knowledge about the Great Temple by watching a video presentation on the Parthenon with examples of reconstructions. Every time I visit the Acropolis Museum, I appreciate the well-presented arrangements of all artifacts by professional curators, who are archaeologists. Still, I mostly enjoyed the top floor's relationship to the Parthenon, seen through the all-glazed façade. It's a tremendous experience. I walked down to the second floor, and when I had finished my tour and photographic endeavours, especially about the lovely faces of the Korai, I glanced across the sculpture hall toward the entrance from the stairs. The masses started flooding the first floor. It was high time to leave.

*

Athens Acropolis Erechtheion Balcony of the Maidens

I took the subway from the Metro stop Acropoli, just off the museum, my mind still filled with the impressions of sculptures I had seen a few times. They stuck to my mind and filled me with serenity. I exited the Metro at Syggrou Fix and proceeded on foot to Marko Botsari Street, looking forward to cooking myself a meal and staying within budget. My muse, Athina, guided me, but why not before as a stranger tried selling me an iPhone that looked suspicious?

I recalled the supervising woman on the second floor of the Acropolis Museum, who enjoyed chatting with me and was interested in my published books. I gave her my visitor's card. Her name was Anna. The image of Anna, the artist, appeared in front of my eyes, but she wasn't in Athens but in Poitiers, France, on a temporary assignment. OK. At least she said it so belatedly to me. And Maria, who still had a collection of my art cards, poems, and personal items, had not yet contacted me. It seemed she suddenly broke off all communication. She had always behaved strangely toward me, except during a painting workshop in Voula, where I had met her in the Art gallery café. Costas, the constant blogger, is on holiday, and around the 11th of February, on St. Valentine's Day, most sweethearts are away. Sending a card and my book to Anna Chara is still a task I'll keep, but probably I'm wasting my time with you, dear Anna.

It's always pleasant to return to my temporary apartment at Kynosargous. I cook champignons with green and black olives, a slice of salami, and some oregano spice on one scrambled egg, which I thinned with milk. It was tasty. This protein-rich dish was followed by chocolate pudding for dessert. Ah! I'll need some strength for tomorrow!

SUNDAY 11.02. St. Valentine's Day.

I'm up early and prepare breakfast: toasted rolls, goat cheese, bread, and fruit sprinkled with Greek halva on top. Mh! I also have a glass of protein drink for a good start, pack my Zeger, and off I go. Just now, I've noticed that today is St. Valentine's Day, and I had planned to travel to Athen's Secondary cemetery in Ano Patissia. I arrive by the subway at Omonia Square, changing the red to green line. The station in Patissia appears to be a bit dismal, especially when I still have to continue on a ten-minute walk to the Second Cemetery along the train tracks, which are not signposted, but thanks to Google, I found the route. Across the railway tracks on a bridge, walk up, across, and down again on the same number of steps. Then, along a long white wall enclosing the cemetery to find the entrance. The porter, who appears limited, calls on a woman from the chapel who listens to my request to find a mass grave for poor people, but her English is poor. I'll type the word mass grave into my Google translator - Ομαδικός τάφος – but she is not responding to that word, except the look on her face says:

I have no idea; I don't know of any here. Perhaps Athina's remark about being excavated after 3-4 years from Athen's First Cemetery and transferred here was speculative. But then, where would her bones be deposited? Possibly at Athen's Third Cemetery?

Athens Church of Metamorphosis below the Acropolis

My friend Mimis' bones were deposited into a place of collection in the same cemetery in Glyfada, where he was buried.

The woman called a priest, who sat behind the priest conducting a ceremony at a Sunday service and asked him about my request. He didn't know about a mass grave either. He said, "Come back Monday at 9 am and ask here at the office. "But," I replied, "why isn't it possible just to enquire by phone?" No answers. "I have tried before on a working day, but nobody lifted the receiver." Modern times. Nobody knows, and nobody cares; nobody lifts the receiver of the official phone. Telos? No, I'll phone the office again tomorrow and ask about the procedure after a burial in Athens. Maybe Athina had been depressed when she remarked about her fate after a burial for a limited time. Probably, I would have been as well.

Back on the donkey road to the tracks, up the steel steps, across the bridge, then down again on the opposite side, and back along the path along the subway tracks to Patissia station. I exit at Victoria Station, the closest subway station to the National Archaeological Museum –

Εθνικό Αρχαιολογικό Μουσείο – 11,000 exhibited Objects from all regions of Greece. All the important finds up to the 20th century were brought here. It is the most v sited museum in the city. Dimitrios Bernardikis, a Greek from St. Petersburg, donated 200,000 drachmas. King Otto arranged a public tender led by the Academy in Munich. Arturo Conti was awarded the prize, and the architect and director of the academy, Ludwig Lange, who had previously worked in

Greece, was commissioned to carry out the work. As the plans were too expensive, the work was postponed. Once the financing was secured, work began in 1866 under the direction of Panagiotis Kalkos. After his death, Theophil Hansen was proposed to continue the work. He refused to build according to Lange's plans, and Ernst Ziller was entrusted with completing the building. Ziller designed the classicist façade. 1940, the museum was closed due to the war; most of the exhibits were buried in boxes in secret places, and the rest were stored in the basement. In 1945, the museum was able to welcome visitors again. At the end of February 2009, the museum was expanded by 24,000 m2 of exhibition space so that 2,000 more exhibits previously stored in the museum's depot can now be shown. The director since 2021 is Anna Vassiliki Karapanagiotou.

The National Archaeological Museum in Athens is the most significant archaeological museum in Greece and one of the most important museums in the world—collections of prehistoric antiquities, Neolithic, Cycladic, Mycenaean, and findings from prehistorian settlements in Thira. In the sculpture collection, the evolution of Greek sculpture from the 7th century BC to the 5th century. AD shows unique works of art. There is a Vase and Mineral collection, metallurgical works, and Egyptian and Eastern Antiquities from 5000 BC to the times of the Roman conquest.

Athens Panagia Gorgoepikoos

The sculpture collection includes metalwork from the archaic period, with highlights including the Kore and Kouros (Ariston of Paros, 550-540 BC), Zeus or Poseidon (bronze statue, 460 BC), Epinetra of Aphrodite, the Antikithera mechanism, the world's first analog computer, about 205-60 BC, and the mask of Agamemnon, a gold death mask of the Bronze Age; the Tombs of the Kerameikos, 460 BC; and the horse and jockey in bronze from 140 BC. There are 16,000 sculptures and 600 Vases. A unique feature is the 'Lady from Mykene.'

This museum, one of the world's largest antiquities museums, challenges visitors to view over 11,000 exhibits, which, in human terms, are impossible to see in a few hours. Still, one's eye will wander around in each room, absorbing the atmosphere and selecting some sculptures for a closer look. The exhibits are selectively exhibited and arranged according to their historical significance, including sculptures and ceramic masterpieces.

For the periods, I started with the Mycenaean period and its rich exhibited jewellery in gold and precious stones, famous for their golden death masks. Continuing with the Classical period of Greek high culture, Poseidon, Hermes, and Aphrodite will stick to one's mind, like the sculptures of Athene and the Korai at the Acropolis Museum.

A man with a 1,5 l water bottle sniggers as I look at a worrier sculpture on a horse. "What's so funny?" I ask h m, but he stares at the explanatory text on the base. My god! I was already tired at the Funerary Stele, and soon, I saw a sign for a café. I need water! Many young girls occupy the space at the counter, asking for a cheese toast and an orange Fanta. I have to be patient, and after fifteen minutes, the sudden invasion of a bee-like assembly has dissolved. But behind me, a queue of fifteen to twenty people had gathered, and their number was growing. The two female attendants, exhausted from the sudden invasion of teenagers, face another arduous task. I receive two bottles of still natural water as I asked the lass in my poor Greek: "dios neras parakalo," practicing some declination. On a wooden seat nearby, I immediately drink the contents of one bottle. I am up again and keen to finish the exhibition. I've been here since 10:00, and it's one o'clock already. I had exhausted my concentration and viewing capacity. Back at Victoria Station, I join the mass of travellers and doze off, landing at Monastiraki Station. Oh yes. I should have changed the lines at Omonia Square. Back again one station and take the red line to Elliniko. At my exit point, now already familiar with, I cross the road the 'Greek way', not entirely on the zebra strip, but right in front of the cars waiting for the traffic lights to change, and walk straight to the small supermarket at the corner to the BP petrol station, and buy a chocolate ice cream cone for Euro 3,50. I walk up the steep road to Markou Botsari 71, wash my hands, doff clothes, take a relieving hot shower, and prepare myself a sandwich. Once eaten, switch on the TV channel Cosmo Jazz at low volume, straight into the comfy bed, and fall asleep. Two hours later, I woke up and wrote in my journal. I prepared a meal: fried sweet potato with some mushrooms and olives—bon appetite. Then, some reading and journal writing. I receive an SMS from my muse, Ina, wishing me a happy

St. Valentine's Day. I replied to her, wishing her the same. I'm glad she thought of me on this day of my pi grimage to find Athina's remains, on this date and year 2024, twenty years since her passing. Where are her remains? I was disappointed with my trip to Athens Second Cemetery, but then I'll ask at the offices of Athens First Cemetery, where she was buried in a temporary grave.

MONDAY 12 FEBRUARY 2024. ATHENS

On a pleasant morning, I'm up early, take a glass of warm water, and switch on the time switch for hot water, giving me a fifteen-minute wait until ready. Meanwhile, I prepare breakfast: fresh fruit and halva with apples and oranges, a sandwich with cheese and olives placed later into the sandwich toaster. Mh! I step into the shower; it's pleasant. It's great to feel clean, like reborn. My hard-on will eventually become an autoerotic sacrifice for Athina. Perhaps crazy, but it feels like saying goodbye to the last remaining physical passion left in me for Athina, completing the healing process during this trip that feels like a pilgrimage. Then, I'll be prepared to go to Ina and get on with our friendly partnership and companionship, being fitting companions for our last phase on this planet. Would I follow up, as I already dreamed and my spiritual demands agreed with Athina, to enjoy her erotically? Did not Athina promise me to send me an intelligent and compatible woman once she had passed on to the 'Big Void'? I have a good feeling I'll find Athina's remains at the First Cemetery and will communicate with her at her last resting place, close by the pompous gravesites of orthodox priests and stars. Have I not visited with her once the First Cemetery and George Seferis' grave? On the way back, we passed the store where masses of bones and skulls were kept by all the people who couldn't afford to pay for a permanent gravesite. It could be visible through a wide window. I completed my breakfast fast, donned my gear, and made a mental note to buy a tee shirt, as I had sweated into the one I had brought along. I walked to the Metro green line, travelled to Syntagma, took the green line to Piraeus, and stepped out at Monastiraki. It's a beautiful morning and a perfect day to spend time at the site of the Agora. I walk through the flea market, but it's not only a flea market but also not an agora. What is it then? A: a MONAGORAKOU, or perhaps B: a MONAGORA, but not a flea market, definitely not. Incredible! The inventive Greeks didn't come up with a more suitable name.

The Agora, next door, is a special place, just like the Acropolis, the famous museums, or the Parliament Gardens. I pay for a reduced entrance ticket in wintertime, but it feels like pre-springtime. A magical sense for a vital temple district, as it is also the place for the temple of Zeus, an altar to Zeus, once busy with buying and selling, but also for rituals to the main gods, the Stoas for the philosophical schools, places for justice and the courts. The oldest temple in Greece for Hephaistos still stands firmly on a hill overlooking the Agora, which has faced the turbulences of history undestroyed.

Athens Agora Stoa of Attalos and view of the Acropolis

In front of it is a strange vision that flickers in my mind: The white sands of crushed Himalayan granite reflect a lake. Yarlong San Poo, or Brahmaputra. It is amazingly foreign but related to the natural destruction of all monuments man has thought to preserve and keep its cultural heritage.

The column drums of the Hephaistheion are sl ghtly dislocated on one side, probably due to an earthquake. Its superb architecture is magical and draws the poet into its ban. My view settles on the Stoa of Attalos' reconstruction by the American Archaeological Institute. Sitting on one of the benches with the mild sun on one's face is a great blessing, thinking back on my visits to a city of fate, enjoying the site toward the Erechtheion and, behind it, the Parthenon, where restorations are ongoing. Architect Kcrres' book *Stones of the Acropolis* isn't available at the bookstore of the Stoa of Attalos, but the sales clerk recommended I contact the Politaio bookshop. I'll do that later. For now, a slow walk along the Stoa, enjoying the busts of famous philosophers and statesmen. Exiting the Stoa and moving towards the entrance/exit gate, a welcome seat at Dodo's Café, watch the world go by, the spray-painted wagons of the Piraeus Metro train below, in a cut-out deepening, with its colourful graffiti. (There's something about it in the 'green journal'. The toilets at the Dodo's Café are clean. The owner has a fable for watches and displays his collection of vitrine items from the 18th century and the remainder of the furniture and cupboards. I walk back through the market and check the shops out. Macramé and handicraft. Mary at shop 120 has pretty hand-painted ceramic boxes for 39 Euros each. However, I bought one ten years ago for half of the price. But I wish to find an owl pin I could attach to the other buttons on my beret. I have an idea of a small silver owl whose material came from the local silver mines. I find a small jewellery shop and talk to the salesman. After a while, he agreed to make up one for me that could be fixed to my beret. He would charge me 24 Euros for it. I have to check my budget and save up somewhere else. He could do it for me the following day. I can't wait to fetch it. Finally, I've found a person who listened to me. Next door to the jeweller, I asked a woman where I could find a shop selling plain tee shirts. She points to a shop ahead that belongs to the same chain. I have selected a white and a black one and paid 15 Euros for both. While I walk back to the Monastiraki Metro station, I think again of a name for replacing the one on the huge banner at the entrance to the market, as I have also discussed with the salesman at the jeweller's shop. I proposed the name Monagora – Μοναγορά – a synergy of Monastiraki and Agora, as it borders on Monastiraki Square and the Agora.

On Day Five of my visit during the second week in February 2024, my spiritual connections elevated me to a new level, so it counts as seven added to day five in the number reduction game, meaning seven, Athina's favourite number and also that she's still with me while I'm wandering around in the great city where we've spent quality time discussing life and love. Has she met with me in spirit? Will she still stir me to hand myself over to her for the last time I might be visiting Athens? OK, I'll take the time when I'm cleaned, showered, and have put on the white tea shirt I bought and get below the warm blankets in the wide bed, writing my journal and see that all experiences are encountered for, needed for my book of lyric poetry: *The Body of the Plane II* a follow up on the first volume, when I was excited to meet her in person for the first time.

I'm tired, but I feel stronger than exercising my legs and feet on days one and two by walking through central town, north to south and east to west. I'll buy some postcards at the Acropolis Museum near Kynosargous and then head home. Mon left me an SMS to remind me to fetch my painting from KVHS/ Spittelau. 'OK,' I SMS her back. I still need groceries, ice cream, a dishwashing liquid, and some tomatoes from the Bangladeshi man at the corner shop, and I will get three tomatoes for 80 cents—then home and shower.

I cooked the remainder of the champignons, using one tomato, some black olives, and one beaten egg stretched with low-fat milk, and made a toast with goat cheese and green olives. MH! It tasted wonderful. Then, I consulted the city map for a walk from Kynosargous to the First Cemetery. As Iannis from the jewellery shop agreed, one would assume that they placed the skull and bones into a central collection room at the same cemetery where one had been initially buried. That's why I'm still carrying on with my pilgrimage. It should be clear to me by tomorrow. The morning will be reserved for that task.

*

INTERMEZZO: NORDIC WALKING along the City Trail No.9 in Vienna's Prater.

Six months later, during a morning exercise, I recalled my wanderings in Athens, which were still alive in my consciousness. It's a Saturday at the end of August. The morning was humid, and my body was covered with a film of moisture. My tee shirt has absorbed the damp condition of the natural moist temperature at Waterfield. Today is my fifth day in the Nordic Walking style along the Waterfield extension's flat area along the Danube. At the start, I had an involuntary sabbatical due to health problems. I had to be motivated to kick-start my sporting walking and return to my usual walking rhythm. Now then, after four days, I had a good feeling of reaching a reasonable fitness level again. It needed the daily exercise for an hour.

Finally, I put on my walking outfit, took my sticks, and headed for the entrance to Waterfield. Along the access road, Wasserwiesenweg (Waterfield Road), I head against Lusthausstrasse (Pleasure House Road). It brings me to the Praterallee and the flyover of the South Eastern Motorway. The continuous swooshing sound of the racing cars above has an eerie quality, especially in the early mornings. I concentrate on having equally strong strides coordinated with my arm movements so my walking will propel me forward, as good Nordic Walking should be. I was taught by an excellent teacher in a Rehab program. Toward the Lusthaus, I walk with rubber covers over the sharp ends of the sticks to reach a smooth performance, even with faster rhythmic movements on the way back on a gravel path.

Athens Agora Theseion Corner Detail

The bridges over the City Trail No.9 are made of steel construction for the trains, painted dark green, while the overhead motorway is constructed in concrete. Further on the home stretch, a colossal bowing tree branch echoes the construction of the steel bridge. Sitting in mind at the Agora, a poem comes to my mind:

Not quite fond of walking this morn'
But mind wins over matter
My feet pulled from a bed of lead
Will break as I run from my mind's
Long corridor of age
When movements are like that of a
Gondolier, arms directing a concert
Of Zawinul and Trilok Gurtu.
I don't feel my body
My feet grew wings of Hermes
I fly below the bridges for trains
Motor traffic and the bowing tree
Branches across the pretty trail of
walkway No. 9
thinking of the rhythm of life and love:
breathing, Sensations of sensuous loving
meditation, and reflection
flying amongst the birds
soaring above the clouds
not too high to end like Icarus
in a sea formed from the dust of
grinding down Mount Pentelikon.
drawing, painting, excelling in making

art like making love
a most exciting way of living.

Meanwhile, I have landed back again from the spot in the clouds. So, the swooshing sounds of fast-moving traffic above the flyover of the South Eastern Motorway wake the rational mind, awakened by the disturbing sounds, the varying speeds of various vehicles, and the singing and spinning tires in this constant symphony of noises. I hear Freddie Hubbard's amazing trumpet solos that almost constantly embed themselves in my mind's discography. I think of white marble and its golden frieze of a meander I chisel as a band of eternal continuation into the castles and rooms I build for myself and my friends and muses.

I'm glad we do not physically feel the earth's spinning or speed travel through the universe. If the genuinely human is the most wonderful thing ever to be developed on this blue planet Earth, how extraordinary is the gift of love to us? we should use it to become better humans! I think of Ina and my wish to lead her to a better relaxation through love, even if it is a one-sided oral act of a man with a woman. That way, she certainly would eliminate the tensions she had built up dealing with the unstoppable wishes of her spouse, who is quite selfish.

Athina said: "Everything we do, we do out of love." Love, the poet mused, as many poets before, what kind or what modes of love are there?

Philia – Affectionate love

Pragma – Enduring love

Athens National Archaeological Museum

Storge – Love for the family

Eros – Romantic love/ The Spark of Attraction/ 'intimate love'

Ludus – Playful love

Mania – Obsessive love

Philautia – Self love

Agape – Selfless love, unconditional love, charity, helping others, good deeds.

Philos – The bond of friendship, brotherly love.

Love - is a complex and multifaceted emotion; how can it be defined with only one word?

EROS comes alive in sexual chemistry and instant desire (From Greek: Erotas). The spark ignites a human being when he or she sees someone attractive. It creates an instant re-action that is impossible to ignore. The ancient Greeks had mixed feelings about Eros. It could lead to intense and passionate relationships, but it also risks losing control. Plato defined it as a common desire to seek ethereal beauty, where a particular beauty of an individual reminds us of the true beauty that exists in the world of forms and ideas.

PHILOS is the bond of friendship. Love exists between friends, showing loyalty, making sacrifices, and appreciating others without romantic or sexual involvement. An ideal love that involves mutual respect and admiration, as considered by many Greeks. It's about intellectual engagement and shared values. This love thrives on equality and mutual benefit, an essential part of human social interactions. Unlike

Eros – fleeting and intense – Philos is stable and enduring, providing a solid foundation for relationships (Iris Dating).

Compassionate Love – includes intimacy and commitment. Deep friendships between couples who have opted to stay with each other but don't have the same intense passion for each other as they may have had when they first started dating. (Sternberg's Triangular Theory of Love).
Intimacy: Feeling connected and close to each other.
Commitment: Dedicated to each other and deciding to be with each other.
The poet had an 'Empty Love' with his spouse of 54 years, but not right from the start. Passion had been one-sided, and desires for satisfaction were selfish from the poet's point of view. When his spouse fell ill and suffered a row of complex health problems, where operative procedures were necessary to save her life. Postoperative procedures isolated the couple. Feelings cooled down for each other, and an extramarital affair of the poet proved his virility; his spouse had denied existed in their marriage, but the boat of his marriage had crushed on the coral reef of the truth about an extramarital relationship that proved to be a lifebuoy for the poet. On the other hand, his spouse had a romantic fixation on her surgeon. Albeit the danger of walking a psychic tightrope and the loss of an intense sexual relationship due to a terminal illness by his beloved, the poet had to pay the price of depression bordering on suicidal thoughts for an extended time. The poet and his spouse experienced love in shades over 54 years, from Eros to commitment and Storge, in an

ebb-and-flow relationship. Light and Darkness. Thunder and Silence. Lightning and Avoidance. Love and Hate. Runaway and Get Together. Did we proceed through the seven stages of love: Attraction, Infatuation, Love, Reverence, Worship, Obsession, and Death? (See: PT-Psychology today, Internet) Well, not yet death, but the poet had experienced his pain and desperation with thoughts of suicide at the passing of his beloved. Would the poet, as a visual artist, experience perspectives of insanity? "Diversity, Equity, ard Inclusion have morphed into Perversity, Insanity, and Delusion." (Carel M Swain).

"By the time you're eighty years old, you've lea ned every-thing. You only have to remember it." (George Burns).

*

Poet's Fervour

Late morn' September's light
Life spirits wake steadily
Don walking gear in grey
And black
Face Weidling's portrait
Lush green vines and
Polished asphalt
Wings of spirit on my heels
Metallic blue sun's reflection
Birds and mice will recognize

In spite of vanished vows
Thoughts intimate, lewd, skin-tight
Demanding with an inner fire
Poems for Ina, drawings for Zed
And singing for the aging friend
There are still birds of thoughts
That fly between the denuded body
Of the poet and the sheer cotton
Film body hugging his sweetheart
Who fluctuates on perfect ripples
Of a body's stone fallen into the
Crystal pond of dusky waters
At the start of another day in
The paradise of their unusual
Bouquet of dark velvet roses
She has pricked her finger on
He'll suck with passionate fervour
The fervour of the unknown
Poet of Love.

NATARCHMU The Youth of Marathonas

TUESDAY 13 FEBRUARY

At 9 am, I'm off to the offices of the First Cemetery of Athens at Logginou Street. I walk from my temporary stay, exit the entrance, and take Markou Botsari Street to the eft, cross to Theodorithou Vrestenis Street, then Trianon, second to the right into Logginou Street. At the offices, I give the clerk the date of Athina's death and read on the page of the Book of Death that her remains were exhumed in 2007, seventeen years ago. Her bones were placed into a stainless-steel box, whose number adds up to six. Now, see, I had an erotic dream about sexual unity with her the day before. Here, I stand in front of her metal box in the store room of the First Cemetery, a simple box for a poetess, unassuming, her bones talking to me and rendering me speechless. She talks to me in a peculiar way that is familiar yet distant, touching my soul. I say something that sounds like a prayer and mumble to her to rest in peace; have I not found you after seventeen years, and have we not met after you were married for 17 years? We still play the numbers game. I can hear her soft, purring reply as if she had expected me at least to do that final act of worship. Another fate-like coincidence with this number 17? Now then, would I return to bring you a dark red rose? Was I tempted to open the box? It seemed to me that it had been opened before, besides by the original handling. A passed lover? A red candle was next to her box, on which the number and her name were written in capitals with a black pen. I realized it was written differently to the name on the cross at her gravesite, with her maiden name first and then her husband's name, but now the opposite. Interesting.

The poet said a prayer, the refrain of a lyric poem *An Unusual Peak*, came to mind he had written for his 'Greek Muse.'

And in the sense of admiration for Odysseas Elytis, he, the artist of exception at heart, just like Elytis, had reshaped his world with words that came from the depth of his being, often as well in noncompliance with the rules of traditional poetry, just as blank and raw as the granite block of the Acropolis, where Classical buildings reflect brilliance and light in a complete culture that flew like a bird into the Western world and multiplied in many variations and imitations.

In the year of her passing, I had written *Athens Elegies* for my mentor and friend, great lover and companion in the arts, besides a continual series of journals and poems. Athina. I visited Porto Rafti before her death, just like Odysseas Elytis had visited this town and harbour a year before his death.

Did this poet travel to Athens this time to find a fourth revelation, when he felt like floating on a cloud of memories, but also with an expectation of a sign for his choice of a new muse he adored for many years and in time his sexual love had developed into steady agape, which in time might become eros? This love could be consumed together, gently, tenderly, and certainly orally, perhaps even sexually, the way his muse would be ready and prepared to whichever degree she could move the measuring stick of her physical performance due to her unique health condition. The poet was sure that she'd enjoy oral sexual attention, as it would not race her blood pressure to exorbitant heights. That would crown life's sweetness in a fifth revelation, one he harboured already for many years and one he had dreamed about and written, also to her through the medium of poetry, love poetry, beautifully worded and laid out as a piece of art. That's his approach to love in literary means reflecting his attitude and care for love, sexually, just like he laid out his lovemaking in his poetry and writings.

But also sitting on a marble block in the Middle Agora and experiencing the powers of an inner relationship, he treasured the most unusual and unique love. Indeed. The fourth revelation that occurred to the poet at times, before this trip to Athens in February, but also during his flight, had been the revelation that he would tell Athina with his body present and in a healthy mind that he had found the intellectual muse Ana-Athina's question confirmed "Is love death," in a near-death experience as a student. Discussing this phenomenon when the poet saw Athina for the last time alive has since remained alive in his mind.

I said goodbye and left my artistic calling card at the edge of her box in the gap of the metallic fold. I walked around in the vicinity of the store. I looked at the mausoleums from white marble, from simple crosses to elaborate gravesites with sculptures and decorations that kept the sepulchral craftsmen and artists in business. I had to think about a photograph I took of her sitting at the gravesite of George Seferis; her head hung, and her face expressed sadness.

I sank into deep thought and then would fathom the depth of this love.

However, Iannis from the jewellery shop in Monastiraki was right: "Ask the office at the First Cemetery, and you should find her bones in a metal box." I replied to him that I had tried several times to phone the offices, but nobody picked up the phone. However, I successfully walked there and used the time to sketch and take photographs. Well, this visit has concluded my past relationship with Athens, which has been living in me through Athina. I won't be able to return to Athens due to my age and the little aches and pains, but who knows?

I continued visiting the Central Market at Armodian Street. The Metro station is Panepistimiou. Go past Ippokratou, into Sofokleous, and right into Armodion Street. I bought Rigani and Nougat, which I'm hooked on—not cigars anymore. I ate an energy bar that helped me overcome tiredness while returning to Panepistimiou station, where I came from.

I found a grocery shop where I bought apples, oranges, and berries. I took a box of pomegranate seeds, which looked juicy and fresh. However, returning to Kynosargous, my box with 'Rodi' seeds was swiped from my Zeger, which was filled up to the top. Damned! The two chocolate bars were stolen as well. "Rot in hell," I swore aloud at the sneaky, stealing bastard in the Metro when I detected the deed.

At four in the afternoon, I returned to Monastiraki to get my owl pin. The owl, a symbol of wisdom, looked beautiful with neon blue eyes contrasting the silver bird. Iannis had to cut the length of the pin soldered on too long. After fastening it to my beret, we had a long talk about creativity and places of instant inspiration, which I found through an abundance of spots of local antiquity. Inspired by meeting Iannis and conducting discussions with the jeweller, a poem emerged in my head. But it came only to light when I resided again in the cottage at Waterfield.

The poet who walks for love
Into the morn's stillness
The Sony clock's tic-tac
Like a nag of consciousness
Seconds become faster.
I'll fly soon at daybreak
Breathe in and breathe out
Oxygen-rich air wooded
Scent close to the Danube
Flood plains, Stadion Allee
Lusthausstraße, roads ideal
For the Nordic Walker
In a way, a Dead Man Walking
Enjoys restarting the tired
Machine's circulation.
My heart reaches out to a
Partner-in-Life, selected by fate
Or, with the help of great, sexy Anne,
Ana, Anetha, Athina?
Feel the power rays of a star in the
Universe, besides beliefs, counts more
Than hard cash in love
When will I see Ina again?
Am I afraid of perishing without

Having enjoyed a last sensuous
Embrace?
ZZ, who walks for Love.

I told Iannis about my inspired writing time sitting on an ancient stone, part of the Middle Agora's foundation walls,
with the mild sun rays on my back and a view of the Hephaisteion. Iannis said: "You are rich." I left, saying goodbye
to Iannis and Monastiraki, and bought some *ξηροι καρποι* –
peanuts with salt, dried out with their skins, which tasted excellent, at the shop *μασουτης* near Panepistimiou Station,
close to the library.

WEDNESDAY 14. February

Today, my morning started slowly for me. I walked to
MOMU, where the local modern artists exhibited, but unfortunately, the museum is closed until 11 a.m. I had to walk
back to the Metro station Syggrou Fix, but I took the arriving
tram instead of the subway. Exiting Syntagma Square, I
sometimes enjoy the sunshine, hiding behind a veil of scat-
tered fine cloud cover. I progress to the warehouse, called
'Public,' take the elevator to the fifth floor, enter the café,
and find a table on the terrace. Syntagma Square stretches
out before my eyes.

Athens Acropolis Museum Connecting view of the Acropolis

My seat is below the open sunshades, and the mild sunshine warms my face. I ordered an espresso and phoned my spouse to share my observations with her this beautiful morning. Visitors gather at the parliament to watch the change of the guards. From the entrance of the substation below street level, a flood of people appears with the rhythm of the oncoming trains. The sounds of a distant humming from the street are recognized by one's hearing, albeit one talks on the mobile phone, and people on the café's terrace are talking on their phones. But in general, the pre-spring atmosphere is soothing to most visitors and locals. I pay and take the elevator to the street level.

Ambling along Ermou Street, I recognize the Byzantine church, Kapnikaréia, positioned like a gem in the street axis, will sit easily in my mind with its ancient. I recall Athina mentioning to me the historic church from the 11th century, built on the ruins of an antique temple. Getting closer, one can see that the sand-brown cloisonné masonry is a masterpiece. The appearance of pseudo-Cufic ornaments is a tradition in Byzantine architecture. They are made of bricks, so the facades have a harmonious, balanced, and aesthetic appearance with a warm colour. It is starkly contrasted with the modern buildings in the development of ten centuries of architecture on this street.

I proceed through the Monastiraki market to the entrance of the ancient Agora, my favourite place for inspiration. I sit down on a stone in the Middle Agora, mild sunshine on my face, and I write, kissed by my Muse's sudden inspiration. I felt tacit that she came to me at the crack of dawn, as I felt touched by her like she used to do that in the past. Well, twenty years ago. So, this is then the twenty-year reunion at her metal box with her remains that were like a relic to me, as I touched her box and left my calling card attached to its corner fold. Now then, I mused later, I never had such a sweet autoerotic experience, and that all of a sudden. There was time for reflection, and I enjoyed my stays at the Agora, writing and musing about my thoughts that projected a slide show of bits and pieces of memory flashes about our times together in love, with the city of central Athens as our play-ground. I felt suddenly tired and opted for my way back through the market to the Monastiraki station. The Metro ferried me quickly to my station, where I walked for five minutes to reach Markou Botsari Street. I had to lie down, slept a bit, and then refreshed with a shower. Dressed and ready to go, I opted for a trip back to the centre of Athens again. I placed a copy of my book, *Walking the City Trails,* a journal of my walking experiences on the perimeter of Vi-enna, into an envelope. I would present it to Iannis from the jewellery shop in Monastiraki and hoped that he'd enjoy it. Unfortunately, he had the day off. So, I left the envelope with the owner of the shop and the lady assured me she would keep it for him. Again, I proceeded to the Agora and wished to walk its entire perimeter. Away from the tourists' trample path, I had to visit the bushes to relieve myself.

I took detailed photographs from the Hephaisteion and sketched some of the temple's corner columns looking up-ward. It's one of the oldest remaining original temples in Greece.

Athens Acropolis Museum Peplos Kore

The aura of its presence has a magnetic effect on one's psyche. I sit at a stone bench and sketch and absorb the view of the nearby Acropolis. I would sit much longer, but I gathered I had exhausted my day's tangible experiences with this historical place where I had spent a whole week diving into the depths of its magic. Indeed! But I could easily continue and stay on if I could find a reasonably priced monthly guesthouse. Perhaps time will tell. For now, I am back at my temporary apartment in Kynosargous. I have to slowly cook my last meal, pack my bags, and head back to my temporary flat in Vienna, or will it be permanent? But who knows? For myself, enjoying an active, creative life as an artist and poet is essential. I have written some postcards to place into the post-box at Syntagma Square's main post office. Great, it's on my way. My Metro ticket for six days expired, so I bought a few one-way tickets at Monastiraki from the ticket machine. At Syntagma Square, I opted for the ticket counter and bought a one-way ticket to the airport at a discount for seniors.

Back at the Airbnb, I checked my Internet booking and decided not to take an upgraded seat. It would have been twice the price of my original pre-booked ticket. I prepared a meal with the remaining groceries and enjoyed the mushroom and pepper combination with a slice of goat cheese. Then, I tended to my journal writing and reflected on my days in Athens.

THURSDAY 15.02.2024

For now: Telos Athens. I got up early, slept well, and prepared my breakfast, but I had less appetite than the day before. However, all packed, and after a welcome shower, I thought of all the items I must take along. What's the word for it? Paraphernalia. That's the word Athina used to say to me whenever we had to leave for the airport or when my spouse and I undertook a trip to the Peleponessos—Olympia and Monemvassia—as she had talked to me beforehand. Now then, goodbye to Athens for some time, I guess.

I left the Airbnb as clean behind as I had encountered it on arrival. The renting lady was pleased. As I entered the Metro, she phoned me, saying, "You have forgotten some things." I saw the photograph she had sent me on WhatsApp: Samaramis' book *The Flaw*, which I left behind as I thought of it as a weak translation from Greek into English. Athina had told me she still had his pipe as a souvenir, and I gathered that she knew him quite well. "So, perhaps you might wish to read Samaramis' book. Welcome." I said to my host. The second item was a white tee shirt I had bought the day before at the market in Monastiraki. "Well, keep it for my return, "I said.

However, I appreciate Modern Greek poetry, especially English translations by American professors for poetry at American universities. I stick to my poetry style, which Athina influenced and commented on, encouraging me to read first-class English translations of famous Greek poets and Noble laureates.

My lyric poetry book, *The Body of the Plane II*, had made good progress. However, it didn't have sparks of excitement like the first one I wrote when I took a flight for my first meeting with Athina. But then, I am very thankful for the emotions caused by this trip after the 20th anniversary of her death when she couldn't welcome me at the airport, and as I was on a quest to find her last remains—the time in the Agora had given me more insight into this unusual relationship of two artists. On an ancient stone warmed up by the morning sun, I experienced inspired writing again that lasted for part of the mornings and afternoons.

Sitting beside a lady reading from her electronic book on the plane to Vienna, I immediately thought of handing her my visitor's card. "Don't be shy, Zeni," I heard Mr T say. "You just have to do your thing, Zolty," Athina told me. Or did I imagine hearing her voice? Using my mobile phone, I came across a statement from Odysseas Elytis: "*If we discover the secret meaning of relationships and penetrate them deeply, we come to a different kind of clearing, namely poetry. And poetry is always lonely as heaven. The question is, from where you can see the sky.*"

*

KORNEUBURG LANDESKLINIK.

After the successful removal of my kidney stones, I felt exhausted, my back hurt, and I didn't sleep as comfortably as I used to. My body's metabolic rhythm had been well coordinated with food and liquid intake before the operation. I sensed that returning to it would take longer than a month. Indeed, after the removal of the stent from my left kidney, I felt elated. Ina suggested swimming, but my body told me to move about by walking.

When I returned to Ina's cottage at Waterfield, I took my Nordic Walking sticks with me. Ina encouraged me to start, and while she used to visit a public swimming pool nearby, I donned my walking gear and started, a bit insecure at first, to take up the rhythmic walking stride that Nordic Walking became famous for.

Ina's cottage lies on the edge of the historic 'Praterlandschaft' – the landscape around the Prater, once inundated by the Danube nearby. However, the wet marshland dried out due to regulatory measures and clever engineering. The troops of Empress Maria Theresia used it as a parade exercise area for the horse regiments.

For the first time, I feel the familiar correct way to stride along and reach the set finishing point at the 'Lusthaus.' It's a good achievement for a mid-eighty-ender. However, for the first time, a set goal is positive, but then repeat exercises for the same distance become increasingly a challenging race for time. Walkers and joggers use music downloads on their mobile phones with Bluetooth technology to uphold their rhythmic movements, not to tire and hold back, but to move forward. I use my mind, and the kaleidoscopic pictures in my mind play me short reels of past and present videos, all stored in the archives of my brain. I see pictures, perhaps as I recorded my day's movements on a separate phone, which is suitable for taking snapshots.

Athens Nat Arch Museum Head of a Kore

Weidling Station: I stand at the Bipa shop, its red sign projecting into the blue and grey clouded sky. An exciting landscape stretches behind the station's roofed waiting areas. Black branches of trees stab into the blue-grey clouds, brown like an emotional sketch design by an artist. It's pre-spring, and the silver lining between the clouds shows the drama of a near rebirth.

My workplace in Weidling: A desk filled with books and journals, green, blue, and red, a tray with colourful markers, pencils, brushes, ballpoint pens, and a writer's desk that collects drawing and writing utensils. I recall the watercolour fixed to the wall of my domain, the HP printer, some thin notebooks in light blue and white, and notes I'd taken for poems and stories.

Next to the watercolour of nudes and flowers affixed to the wall, a print of Schiele's portrait of a nude with boots and her dress wrapped around her thighs lying on her back.

Further left on my wall of paintings is an acrylic work of a muse in the nude with a lover embracing her with one hand. She looks surprised but not uninterested in her lover's approach. Behind the couple is a man's portrait with a black hat and a bluebird with stripes snapping at the rim of his hat.

A book by Odysseas Elytis: Selected last poems by Olga Broumas. I love this book of lyrics with a nude archaic body of a man's back standing at the sea and a shell of a mountainous bubble passing like a boat.

A self-portrait of a serious-looking poet.

Another self-portrait, having woken from a wet dream, interesting the glazed-over reflection in the eyes.

A bottle of liquid Shrooms – Cordy ceps, a mesmerising aphrodisiac.

Coffee pot and kitchenware.

A sketch for a colourful portrait of a muse and artist in yellow, blue, and magenta with an elongated archaic face.

Had the book cover of Odysseas Elytis' poems inspired me to do this?

An abstract watercolour in sulphuric yellow with blue faces, emerald green figures in outline, and the same in dark blue colour at the bottom.

A pic of my bookshelf in my tea kitchen domain, which I constructed with three layers of composite boards on bricks placed vertically with the small faces to the front, but now, six layers would already be needed. But the original idea was to place a canvas quadriptych work above the shelves, and this, besides the sketch, had not yet been done.

A detail of my bookshelf with my published poetry and some manuscripts. Their covers are in white, blue, and also in Bordeaux colours.

An abstract acrylic painting in various blue colours and some yellow-green, emerald green spots, done in 2011, while painting in Athens.

A portrait of the artist and his muses with a white star-ear decor in blue and green.

The last two paintings hang perpendicular to the watercolours on the wall above my writing desk.

A blue watercolour painting of the 'Blue-Line' series features a flying body constellation.

The blown-up portrait sketch of three faces, in yellow, blue, and magenta, affixed to an overhead kitchen cupboard door panel.

The interior of bus 407, travelling from Weidling to the train station, is empty of passengers save for one.

A picture of a Greek meander with seven different designs.

My drawing of a Kore that I admired in the NAM (the New Acropolis Museum) in Athens.

Pictures are jumping into my mind, like Salmon on their arduous journey upstream, as I gaze at the rich greens of the 'Donauauen,' the Danube floodplains, and its reflections in the water of the 'Heustadl.'

A view from the Weidling Station on the platform for the train to Vienna. In the distance, the gothic Twin Towers of the Dome of Klosterneuburg.

Postcard vistas around the station while I wait for the train's arrival. Two dominant buildings at the start of the Weidlingstrasse.

An interior photograph of the old train coach filled with young people, all staring into their mobile phones in front of the coaches' burned orange wall panels.

A colourful design in muted greens and blue colours with an area sitting on a scarlet red flower.

A picture of a round table with the design mentioned before, with a salmon-pink tablecloth matching one flower on the set, a dark green notebook with my integrated emblem on it, a 2024art-calendar from boesner, and my black Lamy pen.

The appointment calendar's open page on the 27ᵗʰ of February, the time I spent writing at Mrs Ina's apartment in Döbling. Of course, *Eros, Eros, Eros*, by Odysseas Elytis' book of poetry.

A photo of the sketch design in red ink of a view of Nero Hill, with the golden dome of the Greek Orthodox Church

In Wiesbaden, I visited with Mr T in 2016 for the film premiere of Drei Söhne, Three Sons, in which he was one of the sons of a father incarcerated in Auschwitz-Birkenau.

A mixed-media drawing in amber and blue. I donated to Mr T in 2016.

A snapshot of Mr T drinking coffee from his favourite cup in grey and white at the dinner table in Döbling.

On a dark, leafy green background are pictures of pretty flowers from Mrs Ina's cottage garden, which are white, purple, and blue.

A photograph of dried rose fruit, a fantastic pic of a sharp reproduction on my apple i12.

These pics serve as a photographic journal and remind one, often triggered by a colour or a drawing, of a walk of visiting my family, as I call it, Mrs Ina's adventures when driving along with me, the museums visited, and the happenings.

I came across the paintings at the famous Albertina Museum in Vienna, where I have seen them at the Collection Batliner. The Collection Batliner:

Manguin's Nude in a Garden.

Paintings of the 'Blaue Reiter'-group. I'm fond of their colours using the same as well. Horses, boats, water and sky, and a landscape with an abstract approach.

Kirchner's portrait of a woman with stark palimpsest outlines and huge expressive eyes.

A portrait with a red background from Yawlensky.

Leger's two women near a boat harbour.

Klee's humoristic picture of a clown and juggler.

Chagall's circus has extraordinary blue colours.

Schiele's drawing of a girl using expressive outlines.

Schiele's watercolours with strained fingers.

Schiele's two women embracing.

Schiele's self-portrait with two models.

Max Ernst's Flowers.

Magritte's Mask on Apples.

Giacometti's Four women on a plinth.

Schiele's Sunflowers.

Avramidis' Medium-sized Figure II.

Moholy Nagy's Abstract Composition.

Marc's Landscape.

Klimt's Witches.

Picasso's Blue Period-Portrait of an Absinthe Drinker.

Next, I visited Joel Sternfeld's photographic exhibition Landscapes in the USA. These are haunting pictures.

I like the Albertina. The Classicistic building is a beautiful cultural container of many forms of art, besides admiring Dürer, Michelangelo, and Leonardo da Vinci, Hieronymus Bosch in the antique rooms, and Grosz in the rooms for the avant-garde artists, where a woman dressed in long black garb has painted her face in a way of a ghosting appearance. All these paintings and drawings sit on my mind, and sometimes some surface clearly, time and again.

Roy Lichtenstein, of course, produced paintings expressing the industrial era with his dot-machine. I have used my self-portrait, drawn on a graphic program on the Internet with a virtual pencil in colours, as an emblem for my literary output and the black-and-white drawings I've done for inserts into my lyric poetry books, *LOVE & ART*.

*

GOODBYE ATHENS

The trip to the airport was lengthy by Metro but economical for my purse. I had to change trains at Doukakis Plakentas. "Wait for the next train," a man told me, addressing me in English. "Oh, thanks!" I was glad to understand the Athens Metro extension to the airport. Still, it was not as clearly understandable to me as depicted on the Metro map I took along when it announced 'Umsteigbahnhof', a station to change trains. A woman who travelled with me with brand new, flashy suitcases and all dressed up complained about the cold weather. "Indeed, "I replied, "Where are you going?" She looked at me and stopped for a moment. "To Mykonos," she said. "And you?" I smiled, thinking about the Greek insular playground for the rich, "To Vienna," I said. She pulled a face. "How nice, but cold." I agreed with a short "Yes." She nodded. Then, our ways parted as she rushed to her flight.

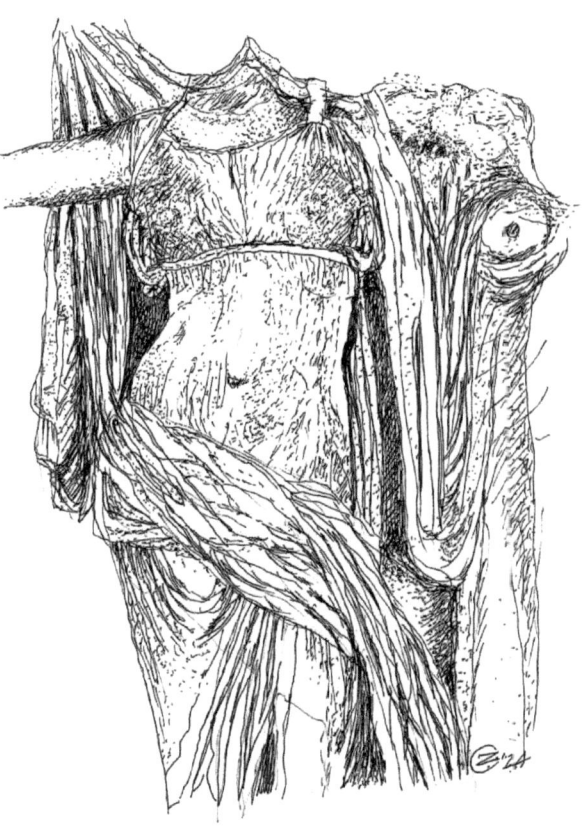

Athens Acropolis Museum Aphrodite

The airport was filled with people wearing similar clothes, a boring same-fashion trend. The young women wear brighter colours than the older folk, and their hair is worn longer and kept simple. I thought about the woman I've known from a workshop of artists before, called Mari. She neither phoned me nor was she reached on her mobile phone. She had kept some of my poetry and artist postcards I wished to fetch. The idea of a mobile phone was to be accessible, but people ignored calls that didn't suit them. So, the book I initially wanted to present to Mari found another person called Iannis. Jo was also unavailable as she was away with a Greek friend celebrating their seven-year friendship so that I couldn't retrieve my Peint-Thole-designed lamp from her. I was disappointed, as I had no budget to stay on longer and felt disrespected and mistreated without alternative solutions to get my goods. I had lost perhaps two associated persons having some valued goods belonging to me from my time as an artist in Athens, but then it consoled me that I had made a new friend. My past friend, Mimis, would have taken my side. Together, we could have won the war of gender and sexes, as it had dramatically increased without any win-win situation.

I am completely disinterested in this silly, competitive-edge approach people are taking. None of my former friends and colleagues has ever tried to assist me in retrieving my art and belongings as if I had voluntarily abandoned them all. Sadly, people I knew well have taken a cold attitude of disrespect for my property. If I had been a Rabbi, then I would have cursed them. I am at war with people, but at least at peace and in love with art! Amen.

*

B, Bee, Bea, Mabea (creative artist in fashion design). Creative in an all-around dressing up, inventing new accessories to every dress she wears. Besides, she lacks a sponsor for a shop of her fashion ideas in Vienna; she walks most of the time along the main pedestrian roads of the inner city and is often asked to be photographed by foreign visitors and fashion-conscious young women from all over the world who appreciate her creative ideas.

She had a hard time digesting the lousy treatment of a landlord in Athens, the disappearance of most of her coats and dresses, the sister of the landlord acquired illegally from her apartment, while the poet had to stay in Vienna. One had to be personally present to sign a registered letter from the province's Social Services to qualify for state support. Tensions for the poet's wife reached their explosive apex when the cash for the household goods she had to sell was wasted by the landlord's sister, Mel, when she changed economically priced return airline tickets for one high-priced ticket from Athens to Vienna, a manipulation that cost the poet's wife energy and took her to near exhaustion. She had to return to Vienna on an unannounced flight, and the poet could not find her at the airport for an hour. Finally, the poet found her collapsed in a common sitting area asleep. He woke her, and fortunately, all her luggage was untouched. He organized a trolley and helped her to catch a cab outside the arrival hall. At their flat, she slept for two days, completely exhausted.

Since then, she has tried to steel herself through regular exercises, heal again from the nightmarish experiences of negativity in an unfortunate situation, and clear a flat of their possessions in Athens, which she had collected over the years, having fallen to waylaying attitudes of her host.

Sports helped the poet's spouse regain her feet and the positive vibes of a most worthy city in Europe, but if not in the world, did wonders for her recovery, and she adhered to the creative ideas she used to compose as installations in her part of the bedsitter. Her hubby, the poet, occupied the other half of the bedsitter since their move from Athens and worked in the kitchenette on his laptop, publishing his poetry and drawings. They had heated debates, even shouting matches and demeaning dialogues, to leave off steam. The poet had an opportunity to render his drawings at the cottage of his muse, Ina, while his spouse, B, could work, without being interrupted, on her ideas at their bedsitter. In time, this arrangement during workdays worked out fine. At weekends, the poet would return, spend time with her, and work on his manuscripts for publishing. This arrangement withstood the times of an artist's frustration. B couldn't sell her ideas, and the poet, fabricating an artistic series of poetry and prose enriched with personal style drawings, could only sell to a handful of repetitive readers. However, he accepted that he would do art for art's sake, while B settled down to wear her creative ideas with arranged clothes and inventive decorative accessories.

Old age crept up on both, and the poet was concerned about their future. Their hate-love relationship continued and changed like the weather patterns, becoming softer and more challenging. Still, the poet had amassed many sketches as a basic skeleton for rendered drawings, canvases, and manuscripts that went back many years. At times, just like B, he would create new literary work, often inspired by Ina, his muse, and the tension of living between a spouse and a love interest splashed off new inspiration for new publications. It kept the poet's artistic ingenuity flowing and his sponsorship from his muse afloat, while B received acknowledgment from a Viennese fashion designer, European travellers, and artistic-minded people.

*

INTERMEZZO Waterfield, Saturday 2024.09.14.

This morning, I was confused. The wind blew, my body felt pain, and my arms couldn't hold the shower rose. Suddenly, I decided to move and get to Weidling. But wind gusts made this impossible as I tried to take the sun umbrella down. I had experienced it day and night, and I thought I might hold out until Monday. I took the rubbish bag to the spot of the refuse containers. However, the plumber had moved his Beemer from the parking lot, standing proud of the other cars, rushed back to his home on the opposite side, and then came back again. "Everything OK?" he addressed me, referring to the new tap he had installed the other day. "Yes," I replied, "but the weather isn't." He guffawed, "Yeah, know it." I returned to the cottage, packed, washed the dishes, made my bed, slipped into my coat, took my holdall and shoulder bag, exited the place, and locked up. Finally, I locked the safety lock around the entrance gate. The walk to the bus station usually took a few minutes, but today, these stormy gusts made it more arduous, and I was nearly blown over a few times.

I felt terrible not having enough strength to take the damaged sun umbrella down and wondered why Ina hadn't phoned, but it was that she was busy and she guessed that I was leaving her cottage, then she would rather wait for me to contact her tomorrow. I didn't feel too well. The new route to Weidling had different times for the Öffis I wasn't at home with for two months when the tracks between Schottenring and Schwedenplatz had been repaired. I took the U3 from Schlachthausgasse to Landstrasse and changed trains to U4 to exit at Spittelau. Here, I missed the train connection of the S40 to exit at Weidling. So, I ambled to the Indian man who gave me four papers for 3,50 Euros. I apologized for handing him small coins. "Never mind," he said. "Thanks," I replied, "my wife enjoys reading." He smiled, and I left and bought two Kornspitz and a ciabatta with provolone at Ströck's bakery. I paid with a hundred Euro note and watched the change pocketing into my grey purse I tried to return into my moon bag. It proved complicated with the three layers of clothing I wore due to the sudden weather changes. I took my bag and the holdall and exited the bakery.

I checked my money, lifted my raincoat, and pocketed my grey purse into the moon bag. Adjusting the raincoat, I noticed I hadn't pocketed my purchase of the rolls and the sandwich. I rushed back and retrieved the paper bags still sitting on the counter. I placed them into my trusted Zeger and left again.

How come I was still that confused today? Was it due to an erotic dream I had that was still hanging on in my mind? I think we like each other a lot, and I want her more erotically than she likes me that way. However, we are good pals and partners for life, indeed. What has happened to me? Something wasn't right. Arriving at our bedsitter in Weidling, having my tea, Ina phoned: "I couldn't get hold of you." I apologized. "I must have moved a setting as I placed it in my moon bag when shopping." She sighed. "I've sent you mail." I replied, "I will look at it." She sighed. "I'll phone you tomorrow, "she said. As I replied, "OK." She was still on the phone. "I have fallen on my face and am not recognizable." My mail opened and confirmed her accident. Another message arrived by WhatsApp and showed a photo of her swollen face. Oh God! What a terrible fall! Many thoughts raced through my mind. Why didn't she take me along, as she mentioned it beforehand? But other matters arose, and I had to stay at the cottage. Darned, I could have watched her step and helped her, even catching her fall, but I should not have chosen a curb with building work to walk on. Now she is in the hospital. I had a bad feeling and felt weak. Now I understand my confusion today. Her vibes must have contacted me at night and during the daytime again. Then I recalled my accident, but I have avoided it to have turned serious. My left foot slipped on the wet step of the bus 77A at Schlachthausgasse, and I fell, but I landed on my left bent arm while the right one held on to the railing. I might have otherwise also landed on my face. Was this a precursor warning of another accident to happen?

*

FLIGHT FROM ATHENS TO VIENNA

On my flight from Athens to Vienna, I dozed off and experienced an artistic slide show on my mind's monitor. I recalled photographs stored on my Apple phone about facades: The minimalistic façade of Athens First Cemetery w th its main entrance with six square and slender front columns carrying a flat roof, possibly with 16 columns in total, in four rows, the pallid blue pre-spring skies in stark contrast to the white marble, the old pavement slabs in grey tones leading to it.

The next façade I recalled was the former castle of King Otto, now the parliament at Syntagma Square, the red-ochre painted walls, the marble frames around windows and doors, and the ten marble columns supporting the balcony above the main entrance and walking towards Ermou Street, turning at the water play of the Square's fountain, an early spring already felt in the warm air.

The neoclassical façade of the National Archaeo ogical Museum has two columns in Ionic style marking the entrance and two corner columns in plain style holding up the classical gable with Acrotiri at the edges and its apex. A pleasantly styled façade rested well on one's eyes as the poet saw it from the edge of the water play at the stepped fountain. The poet sketched its red clay roof to contrast with the ivory-coloured cloud formations.

The façade of the Stoa of Attalos, a reconstruction by the American Archaeological Institute in Athens, with an incredible vista from the end of the Monastiraki market in front of the classical foundation, remains of the Agora. The play of green colours against the white buildings with the Acropolis in the background to this postcard picture. The Metro train with artistic spray paintings passes and cuts through at the perimeter of the site of antiquity.

The façade and building of the Theseion, the oldest antique Doric temple in Greece, between cops of olive shrubs with dusty green leaves against the aged marble colors with orange and light caramel colors of the inner walls, the clouds in a changing formation tossed about by the morning's breeze. The natural appearance of the temple with its six front columns, the slight plaque, and grey stains from air pollution, washed by rain, and vegetation growing between the gaps of architraves. A corner of a column drum was taken away by gunfire, and some drums shifted due to an earthquake, but even all that wouldn't endanger this temple's firm stand on its firm ground base. Its frieze of sculptural depictions is still intact, fighting its decay. From this spot, there's a fantastic view of the Acropolis, its south façade of the Parthenon, its eastern gable visible, the Erechtheion in a dialogue of art, the Sacred Rock with its blue-grey colours against the colours of olive and fir trees of the Agora, the walk along the Stoa of Attalos, the head of a Triton most impressive. I walked alone the entire length of the Stoa, up and down many times, musing about the thoughts that came to me with clarity, cascading into the monitor of my brain. I took my journal and sometimes stopped to record an idea, a picture, and words that came to me and extended to verses of a poem. I was inspired. My theme was love. Hadn't Athina asked me what kind of a poet I would like to be? When I replied that I wished to become a poet of love, she looked at me with glowing eyes. Perhaps she wasn't astonished; I would say that hadn't I sent her the love poetry I had written for her? She nodded and asked me to sit down next to her. Then she took my hand and kissed me. A poetess from a long line of Sapphic tradition had initiated me. I wasn't aware how long I walked the Stoa back and forth, but it seemed that time stood still that afternoon.

*

Athens First Cemetery Main Entrance

CAPT'N

Tall tree of a Capt'n
a head cast in a golden glow
the blue of the sea in his eyes
on the spot to be married guy

Dainty, her sensuous glow
from head to toe, mysterious,
secretive, socialite, and dear
to artists, poets, and scoundrels
Love in separation for months
cannot last, the soul a desert
thirsts for the water of intimacies
voila. Ce ca.

Marriage on the rocks
the seagull's shriek for danger
the scoundrel will bide his time
a silent conquest ship against
the waves.

Beauty against the beast in man
to tempt a boatman against a storm
heaven's weep for a drama uprising.
Earth's black tears flow untenably
the tall tree of Capt'n still stands.

Intermezzo: February 16, Red Tower Room, Vienna. The Poet's Musings.

In the later phase of life, when one feels drawn to a woman, one is drawn to her with a secret wish to be close to her, but the reality in life is not sympathetic to a person in love with another person. He adores his love interest and wishes to hold her close, kiss her, and transfer his feelings of inner happiness to her. One expresses his feelings with physical touches and a stroke on her lower arm, besides smiles and small endearments that make her smile and open her lips as if she would wish to be kissed whenever he makes her laugh. He'd kiss her everywhere, especially to share his excitement. This Friday afternoon, when he met her early in the morning, he thought the day had come that he could be bold enough and follow his desire to kiss her for the first time, but her duties to look after her ailing spouse had priority and then would be a bitter taint that would come between them. "Could you love me?" She once asked a while back, suddenly out of the blue. "Yes," he answered. They would need the right time, the conducive environment, and a special gift from the goddess Aphrodite to become a fulfilled pair of sweet lovers in their advanced ages. They were compatible and, like all women, had an assured feeling about choosing a life companion whom she could trust and feel loved by. B did that, Mischi did that, Athena did it, and even if it couldn't last that long, it was the most wonderful time, well-chosen by my muses. Such are memorable moments in life one holds on to when musing about the meaning of life. However, a one-sided admiration that hadn't turned into erotic love is an advent that later will be remembered as a missing opportunity for love. However, love falls like a seed into the fertile ground of a unique garden lovers must care for and maintain to grow and bloom.

"When we discover the secret relationships of meanings and traverse them deeply, we'll emerge on another sort of clearing that is POETRY. And poetry is always single as the sky. The question is from where one sees the sky." (Odysseas Elytis)

"I have seen the sky from the Acropolis of Athens
And from the Middle Agora, sitting on a stone
In a light that rendered all into a white brilliance
To become one's inner shine." (ZJG)

*

Waterfield Cottage, March 21.

Today is the day of the seasonal start of spring. Having had lunch, I sit on a relaxing chair on the lawn and enjoy the warm sun rays on my face. Some insects have woken from their winter slumber and begun tasting the sprung-up flowers that started before springtime. The rose bush beside me already has lime-green shoots of tiny leaves. The reds and yellows on the bushes show their radiating glow, and although the winter has loosened its icy grip on the greens and the fields, nights are unfortunately down to zero degrees.

Subzero temperatures had nipped the magnolia flowers on the neighbour's tree, and their bright purple turned to brown dead leaves overnight.

The massive trio of high-rise buildings on the opposite side of the Danube channel looks sombre in their dark brown appearance. Finch, Thrush, and Starling warble, but I haven't heard the beautiful song of the blackbird yet. It must sense the oncoming cold weather until the start of April, or perhaps I will listen to its enchanting warble this afternoon. I'm happy here at Ina's cottage, watching the flight of birds and doves with their weighty bodies that are not as elegant as the swallows who flew just now across the cottage's garden. The tiny mossie birds play in the trees, where their leaves have suddenly broken up to grow. The sound of the crows cuts into the delicate general warble that hovers on the KGV's (Kleingartenverein; Allotment Garden Association) environment. A bumble bee hovers on the wild margaritas and the purple violets (Veilchen). It's just a pre-spring start that teased nature's senses for two weeks. Waking up, albeit earlier and earlier each year, is a new phenomenon caused by climate change, but the flies, insects, and spiders could stay away much longer. I caught one with a paper towel sitting on the curtain and set it free on the far side of the garden. The pallid blue skies are cloudless, and jet planes paint long white tails behind their ascendant flight from the airport at Schwechat. Their noiseless ascend draws perfect white lines behind the three gigantic towers where the afternoon sun has settled.

When the birds have finished their early afternoon chatter, one notices the distant hum of the constant traffic flow on the Südost-Tangente (Southeast tangent), a sweeping high-volume motorway bypassing the city centre of Vienna. I've phoned Ina. She's at a restaurant with Mr T, who prefers toned-down Greek food to Viennese taste buds. "Stay seated in the sun, and we'll come to see you within an hour." My spouse phoned me, interested in what my plans were. She prefers town, and I gather she needs company; I can no longer provide her. Our ways have separated mentally and sensually, though we remain friends. How will she see her future? She talks about men interested in her, and I'm glad she finally met somebody compatible with her. I could see Ina as a potential life partner for my future, developing into much more than camaraderie and accompanying escort. Together, we have already proven that we are a good team, sympathetic to each other, have a good middle-class background, and seem to be prepared with consent to walk the last miles of our remaining lives together. Besides, Ina has drive, intuition, and a good head for figures and economy. She's practical and a good project manager, complementing my artistic work and creative endeavours.

*

Recalling the Image of *AnAthAthina*

The Fall

The technicolour of your
battered face by a stirred-up ground
Vermilion – blood's sudden flower
the head's Medusa-hair
free-licking rays of fire and ice
from which new fertile land and
thriving humans are born.
Vermilion – sweet fruit's colour
licked onto the virgin canvas
where libido shapes the unforgettable
twin of the poet's soul.
Vermilion – the poet's vanilla
raising his sugar levels to burst
thro' the plug of a lifelong heap
of an unseen mountain of
chained thoughts
desires of freedom of the mind.
Salt and sugar from the earth
blood like vermilion to the ground
the sudden fall of a weakened and
exhausted carapace.
A colourful assembly of arrowheads
from 85 years on Earth's blue and
green spinning wheel
welcome walking early morn's
twitter of a soul's cleaning

through the rain from the dark
clouds of remembrances
a ray of sunshine
on the clear drying line across
the garden of happy hours
delightful berries of shared
morning meals.
Grey teas of Earls, Counts, Princes
while she swims in a pool of wellness
he'll walk the Prater Bridge to the
island's entertainment paradise.
Licks of apricots from the Wachauer
orchards.
Licks of salt from the Dead Sea.
Licks of love from a poet and artist.
Fine weather at last.
Sunshine smiles upon the flowers.
Garden of Hope.

SEPTEMBER

Waking into the 8,9,10-constellations
date without sweet whispers in my ear
no love without a human touch
calcifications of bone and tissue
legs of burned clay will burst whenever
in a walk towards hope across the arching
Stadionbridge
The once tree-studded street or the
Lime tree dedicated to Franz Schubert?
My desk in the mornings: 100 Love Sonnets,
Athen Architektur und Kunst, from Reclam
Dark chocolate, nuts, sea salt, Nußsterne,
Mobile phone loading
iPhone 12, the photo-handy loading
white plastic bag with medication
thoughts of cross-dressing for kicks
my love interest's top on my skin
the drizzling rain on the fourth day
continues for a 100-year flooding
the alp of drowning in murky waters
yet sunrays, timid and pale through
the breaking cloud covers lie gently
in an eerie, illuminated presence
the red and white oleander shrubs at
the edge of the silver-grey paved
terrace. Waterfield. September.

La saucisse contre L'inquisition (it's about the sausage –
interesting, a crypto-Jewish invention).

Suddenly, he stood at the entrance of a music shop near the
Graben in Vienna. To his left stood a tray with CDs for sale.
He looked through the offers and found a recording of Gus-
tav Mahler's Symphony Nr. 5, with the NJP, the New Japan
Philharmonic orchestra under the baton of Christian Arming;
Robert Schumann's *Tradition and Vision* with Ossberger and
Marantos, *piano for four hands*; and q Wientett: Ravel, Ibert,
Mozart, Barber, and Nielsen. He considered buying it as a
presence for his spouse, who liked Music.
When he took public transport to the pivotal station of Spittelau, he had 20 minutes to spare until the ÖBB-train S40 to
Tulln arrived. Buying two major newspapers from the local
Indian vendor, he contributed to his income, while he also
thought of his spouse, who enjoyed reading certain level-
minded newspapers. Then, with another 10 minutes to
spare, he walked across the arrival hall of Spittelau and entered Ströck's bakery shop to buy two Viennese croissants,
one for his spouse and one for himself for breakfast—time
to go and take the lift to the lower floor, where the train plat-
forms were located.
The S40 train took him to Klosterneuburg-Weidling station in
about ten minutes, from where he waited another five to ten
minutes for bus 401, which took him to his destination at
Servitenhof. He had phoned his spouse before, who had already unlocked the entrance door to their bedsitter for him.
Since the Covid lockdown, he washed his hands immediately

after entering his bedsitter, an essential part of hygiene. He sat down on the green leather couch, enjoying the espresso his spouse had prepared. Having exchanged the news, he got up and presented her with the CDs he had bought. She was pleasantly surprised. "What lovely music...but...our CD player stopped working yesterday. "Oh," he said, "then I'll get a new one." However, she was surprised by the newspapers and placed them beside her reading chair. As an avid reader, many papers were assembled on the low credence beside her reading chair. She began telling him about exciting topics from articles she had read the day before.

*

LOVE & THE CITY
Love, an illusion depicted
On antiquity's ceramic masterpieces
Besides on murals, mosaics,
And paintings, just like cities
On drawings, etches, and on
Engravings.
The city an agglomeration of
Love's labours since antiquity
The belief of creating great
Temples of art to the honour
Of gods, many or one only,
It's not important
But the unity of people and
The state of peace during

Art-activities. Indeed.
Besides the artistic efforts
Of creating something new
And most dramatic for mankind
Like the Parthenon on the
Acropolis of Athens, the temple
As if grown out of the rock.
The artist in search of the spirit
Prevails in the marbles,
The rocky outcrop and its
Sense of space, the
Magnanimous setting, the view
To the Med's Cap Sounion
That reminds me of the black
Sail on Theseus's ship,
The flight of two lovers across
The city that appeared like
Pebbles on the beach
Of Monemvassia, across
The Tower of Winds, the Agora,
The New Acropolis Museum
Furthermore, across the National
Library for a tête-á-tête and
Read about the sanctuaries
Of Eleusis and Delphi.
Back again to sit on a bench
At the Theseion and reflect

Upon the life that started
So incredibly fulfilled, but then
It was so cruelly shattered,
Cut into small pieces of split
I walk upon a unique revisit
And sombre pilgrimage –
LOVE – an illusion.

Waterfield September 26

What caused my irritation? What caused my confusion? Have I looked into the eyes of a lass who served me a macchiato in a small café near the central station? Indeed, I've just visited the laboratories nearby with their ambulatory services, taking blood for analysis. Did I not feel lightheaded? At the age of 84, it could be, but why did I wish for coffee? Ah! I wanted a glass of Viennese tap water that comes with it and isn't charged separately. I missed taking my medication at the service hall earlier. Damned! Wha damned? Because the lass serving me was a young and active person. "Where do you come from?" I asked her in English, as she didn't respond to my German. "From Serbia," she said. It seemed that at this newly renovated Favoritenstrasse Mall, new coffee shops and other retail outlets would establish themselves quite rapidly. Soon, the existing buildings dating back to the last century would be renovated and revitalized. I took a Vimova tablet and flushed it down. I'll pay 2,80 with coins I carry in a black boxlike purse, intended initially for earphones. It fits snugly into my jeans pocket. I left 3 euros on the counter. At the door, I turned my head and looked instinctively back at where I had been sitting, an automatic reaction when I felt like I had left something behind. I saw nothing there and exited the espresso bar into Favoritenstrasse. Further down the street, I checked on the slip I had received from the lab services. Why didn't I notice earlier that I had misplaced my grey keyholder where I kept my folded money notes? Searching for the tram station 18, my stomach started crumbling. I recalled I had a wa nut cookie in my bag and searched for it. As I found it and unwrapped it, somebody said, "Mahlzeit." I looked up and faced a man in his mid-thirties. "Thank you," I replied. "Lunch?" he asked. "No, breakfast," I said. He started to talk about his problems with the local government offices, but I ignored him. "Where are you from? I said, interrupting his sermon. "Serbia," he said. Well now, I thought, first I met a lass from Serbia and now a man from the same country. This must be a district Serbians preferred. My tram arrived, and I said goodbye. I exited the tram station Schlachthausgasse and walked to the Billa store to buy fruit. As I wanted to pay, I noticed that I had no purse. Damned! Had I lost my wallet at Monte Café? And if not, did I drop it when I rearranged my moon bag and the receipt from the lab subsequently? In my mind, I recreated my steps to the lab and then back to the Monte Café, where I did not search for my wallet in my moon bag but took my black box purse with the coins from my jeans pocket instead. I had asked the lass to help open my new medication box, as

I couldn't twist the child-safe top open. She couldn't open it either and took the box to the next room, where her employer opened it. I thanked her, took a tablet, and swallowed some water. While walking to the tram station, I stopped and moved my receipt from the lab from the moon bag's front pocket to the card holder's side pocket, afraid of losing it. However, I still did not notice that I had misled my grey keyholder where I kept my folded bank notes. Only now, when paying at the Billa shop for my groceries, I noticed it was missing. Damned! I had to take a banknote from my reserves. I had to think continually about reconstructing my movements this morning. I took my groceries and walked to the cottage at Waterfield. Systematically, I phoned all the places I had visited that morning to see if they had found a grey plastic purse. Immediately, I realized that if the purse had been found, the notes inside would been gone.

Two days later, when I returned from the cottage to spend my weekend at our flat in Weidling, I opened my laptop and started it as usual. Next to it, I found my grey purse with the money inside. I was elated. My mind's worries and reconstructive efforts hadn't considered that I might have left it at home. Spirited, I carried on editing my book, *Love Revisited, Passages of Love.* The sun illuminated the building opposite my window, and I wondered about my overall body and mind condition two days before. Soon, the incident faded from my memory as I enjoyed the book of Sonnets I wished to publish.

*

Spot in the Clouds

Not quite fond of walking this morn'
but mind wins over matter
my feet pulled from a bed of lead
will break as I run from my mind's
extended corridor of age
when movements are like a gondolier's
arms directing a concert of Zawinul
and Trilok Gurtu.
I don't feel my body
my feet grew wings of Hermes
flying below bridges for trains,
motor traffic, and bowing tree branches
across the pretty city walkway no.9.
Thinking about the rhythm of life:
Breathing, Sensations of sensuous
loving, meditation, and reflection
flying among the birds
soaring above the white clouds
but not too high to end like Icarus.
Drawing, painting, excelling in making
art like love
a most exciting way of living.
Meanwhile, I've landed back again
from the spot in the clouds.

A Reflection Like a Prayer

Ana, Aletha, Athina
The A's like body, mind, soul
At first, curiosity; some saying
Goes: Curiosity killed the cat.
Indeed.
Secondly, the trend of experiencing
A girlfriend online that may lead
To one's good luck of love on
The Internet – the thrill of intimacy
With a stranger, it goes for both
sides. These meetings to chat
lead to the exchange of sensual
feelings, a first for artist and muse.
Learning to know each other on
A fast-track tête-á-tête
Meant soon to know a person
Better than his spouse of
Thirty years.
The desire to denude someone
Seducing in full view on a screen
Is exciting and spills petrol
On the fire, one kindled.
Exciting for both partners, who
Are compatible with similar
Libidos, same interests in erotic
Love and the arts. In poetry.

Both lovers with matching bodies
With similar spiritual leanings
Believes in fate and fulfilling
Their human needs.
The artist who leans toward
Poetry helped to develop his art
By a poetess, his muse and
Teacher. Inspiration thru' love
And fights for one's beliefs and
The control of jealousy flares
Seeing one's beloved embraced
By another woman.
The meeting in flesh and blood
As star-crossed lovers, not yet
Known to the poet, the artist,
The friend, the lover, mother,
And spouse.
Love like there is no tomorrow.
Tale love physically possible
To test the personal limits?
Did not the poet's spouse state
Repeatedly, he never could
Satisfy her? But why could he
Satisfy his muse online, in her
Arms, standing, and chafing,
Lying and changing positions
Becoming an oral well-oiled
Lover? Damned!
Pity for his muse, it's the

final curtain.
Was it that she still wished a
final love of body, mind, and
Soul?
Did she sense that this artist
of her choice would be the
right partner for her final fling?
Was it though a fling that
turned into love and tears
of joy?
Was it then that the artist
could finally be sure to satisfy
a sensual woman?
While both partners were seeking
the truth and being lucky as
compatible partners to find
their ways forward: The artist
discovered ways of expressing
the state of his soul with words
and in drawings
his muse would become a woman
again, after seventeen years of
a stand-off in her marital life.
But her untimely death as a
great love drove the artist to
the edge of an abyss to jump from
Lover's Leap on the Acropolis
the drama of star-crossed lovers!
Yet, his muse had sent him another

love and another, and yet
he couldn't love them as he
loved An, Ane, Ath – so he reflected
wrote, drew, and published his
lyrics, drawings
his experience became a
metamorphosis of love that
changed everything, healed his
jealousy and placed him above
pure desires and egotistical
projections.
Love heals everything.
Is love death? An, Ane, Ath said
before she left the blue planet
to return to the universe.
The poet mourned for years
but also enjoyed the floodgates
of creativity in all its pure colours
he applied to paper and canvas
expressing a world-changing event
in his life.
Reflecting. Musing. Enjoying his
new muse he feels at home with.
A reflection like a prayer in
three ways: Body, mind, and soul.

**In art, as in life, anything is possible if founded on love.
Marc Chagall.**

Waterfield Friday, December 13.

We talk daily on the telephone. If we don't speak, I feel left out of our delicate bond of friendship. Experiences with relationships of love surge my literary output. Lately, however, we have looked back on our lives and found common ground in most matters related to our aging conditions.

I met them while I was helping Mr T in his art shop. Befriending Mr T's quicksilver assistant, Nica, who presented herself as a religious woman, Mrs Ina appeared a great mind behind her husband's endeavours, placing the oeuvre of his late father on the international map following many years of exhibitions all over Europe. Whenever I couldn't help Mr. T, and he needed care for health reasons, Mrs. Ina would ask me to assist her with caring for her father-in-law's oeuvre; I learned to know while working in a rented, well-ventilated, and secured depot. During this time, I felt closer to Mrs Ina. Had fate presented me with an outstanding Muse? Has she been sent to me by my past muse, Ana, who had to part from this planet? Even if it had been just a pleasant thought, a terrific wish for me to carry on my creative work, Ana had cared for me with a continuation of inspiration an artist would need and only a muse could provide. However, one thought about love and death remained: Love in all its facets and appearances.

One late morning, while working at the artist A. Frankl's paintings storage facility, Ina asked me to join her at a nearby Anker bakery for tea and scones. Her behaviour seemed different this morning than on the other days during the year. When we were seated, she opened her bag and took two colourful strings out. "These are friendship tokens," she said in a low voice and asked me to extend my arm. She fastened one of the strings around my wrist and then handed me the second one, which I fastened around her wrist. An important and unique moment happened this morning: I was part of a ritual that reflected our closeness through these colourful bands we tied each other's wrists. It became a continuation of my friendship with Ana, love between friends, the start of a relationship spoken out between us that happened through the times of my assistance with Mr T's Art shop, followed by my continued personal assistance for Ina, the name I call her in my poetry and a relationship I had wished for. Could love between friends grow to more intimacy? Indeed, I've projected my desire for love besides touches and kisses to eroticism, which we exchanged at times with first touches and a subtle physical nearness. Being married, I respected Ina, and she did the same. As the poet who lived in a world of closeness to his muses, she became my muse many years back when we first met, and she had asked a friend of Mr T, who spoke to me, what I would charge for a portrait of a woman, but as her husband was jealous, she couldn't sit for me, but I could use photographs. Later, I gathered that it could have been Mrs Ina who wanted her portrait painted. Circumstances drew us closer together. Years later, Ina's husband complained about us spending more time together than she would with him. I smiled inside, unaffected by his jealous outburst, "She is still my wife!" I agreed with him, "Of course." I noticed a faint narcissistic smile around his curling lips. It wasn't different with my spouse, as I observed a significant similarity in their attitudes toward my friendship with Ina. While we, the quartet that would stay in limbo besides our friendship and love, noticed that we'd entered a circus performance balancing ourselves on a highwire act in relationships, my mind reflected this in the series of blueline drawings Ina named. Had we not felt a growing closeness being birds of a feather but walking along a path that bonded our souls? Did she not call our friendship a final act of mature love?

For Ina's birthday in her eighties, I drew her portrait of a stage when she felt at the apex of her life. I used a nuanced photographic portrait I liked as my inspiration. "Yes," she commented, "it looks like me." She hung my drawings and paintings in her new domain, which she had designed to suit her style. She honoured me. While I felt committed to her friendship, I have been drawn at times physically to her, but then I sensed Ina drawing back. Not that she wouldn't like to live it up with me, but aesthetically, she had scruples that would make us disappointed in each other. It wasn't the age factor, as we were both physically still reasonably good-looking, but it seemed to be wise not to fall into the tender trap while our spouses were still alive, and we had our reasons for not going through the pains of a divorce. That could be technically easier for me than it would be for Ina. However, being in the mood for love would come to us one day, without any stimulants, just at the height of happiness at a place that suited us both. I felt it in my heart. Probably, she did think that as well.

To be together most of the time and not telling our spouses meant to have ties of friendship, but the pending wish for intimacy that hung like the sword of Damocles when we were together. While Ana had been concerned about love-sickness, "I'm sick of love," which we both felt in all its intensity. Still, she said, "You love me more than I love you," perhaps right as my libido drove me to her irresistibly. I couldn't get enough of her, with libidos intact, which had been a natural development with falling in love with a compatible and good-looking couple interested in art and literature. Ana shaped my road ahead, influencing my literary output and putting me on the road of poetic expression by accepting me as a poet and contemporary writer spurned on expressing my love for her.

When Ina decides to have time, we share lunch and amble down from her apartment across the centre of town to our favourite café, where the prices aim to support the creative folk, the humble artist, actors, and playwrights. Photographs of famous actresses and actors adorn its aged walls. She sits on a wide, comfortable bench, and I sit opposite her. I look into her blue-green eyes. The play of eyes gives me hope for a fine future together, 157oweverr long or short-lived, with much love that just has missed the passionate years back, but then she might have preferred female company, while I preferred my artistic endeavours. Well, we still have a friendship that counts for much more. Or?

*

Love lost and found

The one love I've lost
that still feels to be irreplaceable
while the sun comes up thru' the
mechanics of the universe
burning on my skin like the love
once lost.

Stepping out cautiously like a camel
on the dunes of a sea of sand
sensing the traps of life's quicksand
while the journey thru' gold and
lemon colours continuous –
travels by train along the Danube's
rising waters sweep your portrait
along a boat of intense thoughts:
Love, defined by thunder and storm
by the depth of the ocean
the peaks of the Himalaya mountains
the cracking sound of a jetfighter
passing the sound barrier.
Love lost between the pages of
Lyric poetry, between the lines of
sensual drawings in the shadows
of the maidens on the balcony
of the Erechtheion.
Yet, there's still a new dawn rising
above the spicy morn's of Waterfield
cottage's greens, hibiscus opening
her receptacle bloom reminds me of
your dormant love
you have shielded from me since
the years of love that had to be
patient, like the metamorphosis of a
butterfly.
Then, since you've given me wings
of intuition, touches of a caring friend

love has grown with awakening senses
a woken-up patient from the dreamland
of women and men mending my shell
and restoring the flight path of my
destiny.
I'm grateful you hold my life in your
hands, your soul that knocks on the
door of mine, for I'm hungry and eager
to taste the white blood of your being
in love's fading embraces.
Love, embedded in the mechanics
of the universe.
Love lost and found.

Waterfield, Saturday December 14.

Le weekend. Again. Time seems to race past me like a speed train. My time, which I spend from Monday afternoon to Saturday morning, is over.

I spend Saturday and Sunday until Monday afternoon at our temporary home in Klosterneuburg-Weidling, a quaint village with no life at all. It's all right for a poet, artist, or writer, but it felt like a prison for my spouse. Unfortunately, air pollution produced by the growing volume of through traffic along the main road nearby and cars by neighbours driving to their doorsteps, traffic fumes from exhausts and bad tires results in fine dust pollution that settles not only at our doors but also inside the room. Cleaning the bedsitter becomes a nightmare.

Black spots on the laminated wooden floor seemed to be of an oily substance if rubbed between one's fingers and reminded of the soot from the industry. We observe the rising traffic with heavy lorries for hauling wood logs from the nearby woodworkers in the Viennese woods. Tank lorries with sewage extracted from homes and farms where the local council hasn't yet extended the underground sewage system. Living in a depression toward the Weidling brook, the polluted cold air from diesel exhausts will drift down towards our flat at ground floor level, where adjoining tenants from across a shared yard regularly drive their cars to park outside their apartments. A tune-up mechanic has rented a garage next to our flat, and although he is using the extraction fan in the garage's basement, tuning up sports cars becomes annoying, especially to my spouse, who is closer to the source. At the same time, I work on my laptop in the kitchenette behind the bedsitter with a closed window that reduces the noise level to a humming. Fortunately, the hobby mechanic turns up once a week.

It's not the only problem my spouse is facing. A family of three recently moved into an apartment in the opposite building, about 15 meters from us. Although the husband generally behaves in an educated manner, he is constantly on the move with his car and a grey Merc, which he uses like a working donkey, and at times, he arrives with a canvas-covered trailer he disconnects in front of our entrance door and then pushes the trailer into his locked-up garage. In contrast, the cars remain in parking spots outside. Besides, while his car is often absent on weekends, his wife travels back and forth to shop for groceries; she then takes one by one from her booth to her apartment upstairs, with the engine running. This seems to suit her, but the exhaust fumes pollute the air. The same goes for mornings when she warms up the engine and the exhaust fumes land at our doorstep, rendering the door folds black. Lately, her husband joined her in letting his car's engine run for five to ten minutes. When my spouse asked why he did this, he replied, "The car has to load." Does he mean to run up the engine to running temperature? I said to my spouse. But it's an attitude that means he treats the commonly used yard belonging solely to him. Due to its limited size, I thought the yard should be neutral ground for all tenants and, therefore, shouldn't be used as a day-to-day parking facility. But it was a selling point for the landlords, as parking remained limited even in this village. The renting agent had warned us about renting this bedsitter, but we had no choice at the time to secure a reasonably priced apartment for two. Lucky to have found this accommodation, we discovered affordable rentals are still as limited as many years ago.

Thank God for Waterfield, an artist's paradise where I enjoy the peace of mind and tranquillity of a green lung while living close to the city. I'm in good luck knowing Mrs Ina, who owns this treasured cottage she renovated. I write my journals and poetry here and create my drawings for insertion into publications. I am lucky indeed to be making friends with her. Having good friends, I've earned their respect for my art and writing, and while they support my artistic endeavours and my stay for up to five days a week, I am grateful to Ina for letting me live out my creative activities here at Waterfield.

*

About the author

Born in eastern Austria, close to the Hungarian border, he witnessed as a young man the horrors of a nation's suppression erupting in the Hungarian Revolution of 1956. He finished his education in art and architecture in Vienna, married, and sailed for the Cape of Africa, an adventure that followed his childhood dreams. He had drawn African animals for his art classes, but the time had come to see them in their natural habitat.

Meeting a varied facet of people and cultures, working as a draughtsman in an engineering office, and as an architect for a cultural centre, he made good use of his language skills travelling throughout Southern Africa.

During a trip to Lesotho, a native artist showed him rock paintings with their stark palimpsest outlines and with typified movements of animals and humans. It made a lasting impression on him and influenced his artistic work.

His vast collection of drawings and slides had been lost during a change of domiciles, but further studies of the San people would reawaken his dormant artistic longing for the expression of his art, filling sketchbooks with drawings and notepads with poetry and prose. While revisiting the capitals of Europe, he sensed that the bond of art, being borderless and free, would reach out across continents into the world. During a visit to Greece, he was accepted into the circle of artists and poets who encouraged him to continue his art, and a poetess introduced him to the works of famous Greek poets.

In South Africa, he joined the writing and poetry workshops of *Writers Write*. It was to open the floodgates of his creativity. He decided to travel through Greece and visit its sites of antiquity, read up on Classical mythology, and enjoy first-class translations of Greek poetry and prose.

He settled in 2013/14 in Klosterneuburg-Weidling. Poet Nikolaus Lenau is buried here. Franz Kafka had visited here. Their writings will always be an inspiration.

*

Other books by the author

(Available at BoD-Books on Demand/bookshop, Norcerstedt, and all major bookshops, as E-book or in print)

In English:

Acropolis – Book I, Fervour

Athens Elegies – A Poet's Lament

Cantos Libidos – Love's Pure Emotion

Clouds I – Dancing Eros

Clouds II – Wing-Child Eros

Diary of an Aged April – a month in the life of a poet cn the
Southern hemisphere

Educating Pizzy – The Artist Evolves

Elegy of an Unusual Peak, Book I – Real and Virtual Loves

Elegy of an Unusual Peak, Book II – Days in Love

Fighting Stance – Triangulation in Love

King of Ice – A Poetic Legend

Love Revisited – Passages of Love

LOVE & ART – Songs of Passion, First Volume

LOVE & ART II – Songs of Passion, Second Volume

MUSES – The artist between heaven and hell

MUSES II – The artist in the Muses' Garden

MUSES III – Waking in Love

MUSES IV – Magic Unisons

Poetry in times of lockdowns and isolation, Book I –
Missing the City's Hub

Poetry in times of lockdowns and isolation, Book II –
The City Deserted

POETRY OF THE INNERMOST Book I – Colour Scales of Love

POETRY OF THE INNERMOST Book II – In Praise of Mature Women

Red Tower Room – A Poet's Refuge

In German:

*

References

TheAcropolis, A guide to the monuments and the New Museum
Dr.G.PapathanassopoulosKrene Editions, Athens.

Reclams Städteführer Athen, Architektur und Kunst
Klaus Gallas.